The Bonds of Friendship

First Edition

Published by The Nazca Plains Corporation
Las Vegas, Nevada
2009

ISBN: 978-1-934625-98-9

Published by

The Nazca Plains Corporation ®
4640 Paradise Rd, Suite 141
Las Vegas NV 89109-8000

PUBLISHER'S NOTE
The Bonds of Friendship is a work of fiction created wholly by *Lew Bull's* imagination. All characters are fictional and any resemblance to any persons living or deceased is purely by accident. No portion of this book reflects any real person or events.

Cover Photos, IStockPhoto
Art Director, Blake Stephens

Dedication

To Tony and Mark,
Your bonds of friendship have encircled me with love and care,
and for that I am indebted to you both.

The Bonds of Friendship

First Edition

Lew Bull

Chapter 1

The wooden base of the double bed creaked as the tall, slim, naked youth slid from under the warmth of the duvet and padded his way to the bathroom. He turned on the tap of the wash-hand basin, splashed his face with the running water and then looked in the mirror. The fine features looked back. He smiled at himself in the mirror and the high cheekbones became emphasized. The lips were full and looked lascivious. He ran his index finger along the length of each eyebrow, following its curvature; every hair seemed to be in place.

"Selwyn, are you making tea?" came a voice from the bedroom.

"Are you awake?" was the reply from the bathroom.

"Yes. What are you doing?"

"Just admiring myself in the mirror to see that everything's still there."

A chuckle emanated from the bathroom.

Selwyn made his way from the bathroom through the small apartment and into the kitchen. He switched on the kettle and allowed it to start humming as it boiled the water. He took two mugs from a cupboard and placed a tea bag, plus a drop of milk in each and waited for the water to boil. Once the water was ready, he poured it into each mug, letting the tea bags draw and then withdrew each bag when he thought the tea was strong enough, gave each mug a stir and proceeded to pad his way back to the bedroom once more.

"Morning my love," he said bending over to give his partner a kiss and putting down a mug on the bedside table. He then went round to his side of the double bed, placed his mug on his bedside table and slid once more under the duvet to the warmth that exuded from the body already in the bed.

"What are your plans for today, Selwyn?"

"I thought I'd just tidy up the apartment and then maybe go to for a swim," replied Selwyn, snuggling closer to his partner. "What time do you think you'll be back from work?"

"I should be back by 5:30 at the latest, if I don't have any appointments."

Selwyn put an arm around the warm body lying next to him. It was still early and the sun hadn't risen to warm the earth yet, so Selwyn was reliant on body heat to warm him.

"What are you after?" came a quizzical voice.

"Nothing, but a bit of warmth before you go to work; but of course if there's a bit extra, then that's a bonus," he giggled.

The two lay in each other's arms feeling a glow transfer from one to the other. After some time, just before both dozed off to sleep once more, a rather tired voice said, "Selwyn, I must get up and get ready for work."

Michael threw back the duvet and hung his legs over the side of the bed, stood up and went through to the bathroom. Selwyn lay there admiring his partner's firm, naked, white ass, as he departed from sight. The difference between Michael and Selwyn was that although both had a tanned color to their skin, Michael had a white ass while Selwyn's was the same color as the rest of him, and it wasn't from tanning in the nude. They had recently met when both had been on a night out to a local club and Michael, being a little drunker than usual, had swept Selwyn off his feet with charm and drinks and taken him back to his apartment where Selwyn had remained for the last two weeks.

Although it was a small apartment, in comparison to some, Michael had partitioned off the lounge/dining area with a folding screen made of white louver slats, allowing for a modicum of privacy. The furnishings throughout were simple but practical, with a two-seater couch, an easy chair, a coffee table and a couple of side tables in the lounge area, and a four-seater round dining-room table with chairs in the dining area. Décor wise, apart from the odd ornament, and odd being the operative word, there were plastic and silk floral arrangements scattered around the apartment making it resemble a funeral parlor. The reason for this plasticity was Michael's love of gardening and the inability to have a garden in his fifth-story apartment, so the next best thing was to bring the floral kingdom indoors by means of these dust collectors.

It was probably his love of the outdoors that led Michael to his profession.

Michael was a real estate agent whose hours of work were erratic, which meant that there were times when he'd finish work early, but it also meant that he might have to take out clients in the evenings, or it meant that he could come home all hours of the day when he didn't have appointments, but Selwyn, on the other hand, was unemployed at the moment, which meant that he had all the time in the world to do as he pleased. When I say unemployed, I don't mean that he never earned an income! But more about that later.

Michael showered, dressed for work and made himself some breakfast, while Selwyn chattered freely to him, following him from bathroom to bedroom, to kitchen, to the small round dining-room table in the lounge area, to the front door.

"Bye-bye babes," said Selwyn giving Michael a kiss. "Have a nice day and I'll see you later."

Michael left and Selwyn immediately went back to bed until it had warmed up outside. However, Selwyn dozed off to sleep after Michael's departure. At 10:00 the telephone rang, waking Selwyn from his slumbers. He stretched out for the receiver and the dreamy voice answered.

"Hello."

"Hi Selwyn. I just phoned to see if you were up yet."

"Oh hi Michael. I was fast asleep when the phone rang. What's the time?"

"It's 10:00; time beautiful men should be up and about. I was wondering whether you'd like to join me for lunch today, that's if you're not doing anything other than going for a swim."

"That sounds great. What time and where?"

"Be at the apartment by 12:00 and I'll come round and pick you up. OK?"

"Sure," replied Selwyn. "Then I'll see you later. Cheers for now."

Selwyn replaced the telephone, stretched and eventually slid from the warmth of the bed. He began to dress for the swimming pool, pulling on a bright yellow Speedo that seemed to become enhanced by the color of his skin, a pair of white shorts over his Speedo and a pale blue T-shirt. He slipped his feet into a pair of sandals, picked up a beach towel and left the apartment to make his way to the nearby swimming pool. Their apartment was only two blocks from the public swimming pool, so the stroll didn't take long.

On arriving at the pool, he found a vacant spot, laid out his towel, stripped off his shorts and T-shirt and lay down on his back to tan in the blazing sun. He had lain there in the hot sun for about three-quarters of an hour when a strapping man of about early forty, strolling around, approached him.

"Morning. Nice day for tanning," said the man, standing and blocking out Selwyn's sun on his body.

"You're standing in my sunlight!" said Selwyn, shooing the man away so that he could catch the sun's rays again; but the man remained standing where he was.

"I thought I was doing you a favor by blocking the sun from your eyes," replied the man, now lowering himself to sit on the edge of Selwyn's towel. "By the way, my name's Greg."

"How do you do, Greg," replied Selwyn, rather formally and indignantly, but without giving his name away.

"Nice tan you've got there. Do you come to the pool often?" asked Greg.

"Thank you. I come as often as I can," answered Selwyn, casually but with a double meaning to his statement and a twinkle in his eye.

There was a pregnant pause and then the man spoke again.

"Excuse me saying, but you've also got a very nice body."

Selwyn felt flattered, but wasn't about to take the bait, so he thought for a while and chose not to respond. However, the fact that he'd taken the trouble to hold a conversation with this stranger meant that he'd already taken the bait.

"Do you go to gym?" asked Greg, slowly inching further onto the beach towel.

"No," replied Selwyn, trying to act nonchalant.

"You could have fooled me," laughed Greg.

"I've just been blessed with one of those bodies you know," continued Selwyn.

Greg sidled up to Selwyn's right leg and, touching it with his hand said, "You've got great legs; long and muscular."

"Yes, and so did Colossus have great legs," replied Selwyn. "The only difference is that he stretched his across a harbor and I stretch mine around the harbor."

Selwyn had decided to be forthright with this stranger, but for some reason, known only to Selwyn, he never moved his leg away from Greg's touch, instead he allowed the man to leave his hand resting casually on his thigh.

Selwyn noticed how Greg constantly smiled at him and occasionally squeezed Selwyn's thigh where his hand was resting. Selwyn also noticed that a familiar type of bulge to his own was growing in the front of Greg's shorts that he was wearing. Having this man touching him was creating a feeling over which he had no control. Should he flip over onto his stomach to hide his embarrassment, or should he remain lying facing Greg? He chose the latter, being a bit of an exhibitionist that he was.

"That also looks good," continued Greg, staring at Selwyn's yellow encased crotch and sliding his hand a little higher up Selwyn's thigh until it reached just short of the growing bulge.

"I don't think you should be touching the goods out here in the open at the pool, after all, this is not the open-air market," remonstrated Selwyn, trying to take control of the situation, but still not flipping over onto his stomach.

"Have you got somewhere we can go?" came the instant reply.

Selwyn was a little dumbfounded by this. Here was a man coming on to him, an act not foreign to him, yet a few kilometers away in an office was the man in his life, Michael. Here was a dilemma: on the left shoulder sat a little hypothetical devil saying, *'take this man home with you for a quickie'* and on the right shoulder sat an equally hypothetical little angel who said, *'refuse his advances and tell him about Michael.'*

"Oh, shit, here we go again!" muttered Selwyn, with the devil prodding his left shoulder. "Would you like to come back with me, but it'll have to be quick." The devil smiled.

"Do you stay far from here?" questioned Greg.

"No, it's about 200 meters from here. Shall we go?" said Selwyn, rising rapidly from his towel and wrapping it around his waist to hide his erection, then slipping on his T-shirt. He picked up his shorts and towel and the two of them headed hastily back to the apartment.

When they reached the apartment, Greg was ushered in and both he and Selwyn went and sat at the round dining-room table, only because Selwyn wasn't about to make for the bed straight away as he wanted to find out a bit about this man, before the action started, so Selwyn discarded his towel and sat back, relaxing.

"Do you live alone?" enquired Greg, surveying the place.

Dilemma number two. Does Selwyn tell the truth or does he concoct some other story?

"I share the flat with another guy," came the response, after a little prodding from the angel.

Very non-committal! This guy that he shared with could be his brother, his landlord, his father, or in fact any one he wanted it to be, other than his boyfriend.

"Oh. But are you in a relationship with this guy?" asked Greg, trying to ascertain the relationship of this person to Selwyn, who incidentally, had still not revealed his name.

"Yes, we're good friends."

"Well, would you say good friends or GOOD friends?"

"Well, when you say it like that, I suppose you could say we're ...." Prod, prod from the devil. "Yes, I suppose ...GOOD friends," replied Selwyn, having received a sharp prod from the angel and being not quite sure whether he'd now put Greg off from his earlier advances. "Does that worry you?" continued Selwyn.

"It doesn't worry me as much as it might worry you."

As they sat discussing, in subtle ways, whether Selwyn was doing the right or the wrong thing, they heard a key being inserted into the front door keyhole.

"Fuck, it's him," hissed Selwyn. "Quickly, under the table."

Greg, without hesitation, scrambled under the round dining-room table while Selwyn pulled the long table cloth over its edges until it reached the floor in order to cover Greg's hiding place.

"Just keep quiet," whispered Selwyn.

The front door opened and in walked Michael.

"Hi, Selwyn. Have you been to the pool already or are you still going?"

"Why are you home so early? You said you'd be back at midday."

"True, but our morning appointments were cancelled, so I could come home earlier."

Michael pulled out a chair at the dining-room table and sat down to talk to Selwyn, unaware that Greg lay under its covers.

"So, did you go to the pool?"

"Hm!" muttered Selwyn, nonchalantly.

"What was it like?" asked Michael, stretching across the table to take Selwyn's hands in his.

"Not bad," came the carefully worded reply.

"Meet any of your friends down there?"

"No," replied Selwyn, shaking his head, and receiving a sharp jab in the shoulder from the angel. "No, I wandered around until I found a fairly sheltered spot and lay there for a while."

"I hope that nobody molested you while you were there."

Selwyn shook his head as if to say that he hadn't been molested. "No, more is the pity," added Selwyn, giggling as he said it.

Selwyn suddenly froze as he felt Greg's hand rest on his upper thigh, under the table, and then slide up towards his Speedo encased crotch. He felt a finger run over the smooth material and could also feel the start of a burgeoning between his legs. The smile on Selwyn's face grew wider and wider as Greg's fingers slid around his crotch under the table.

"What's the joke?" asked Michael, noticing Selwyn's smiling face.

"I was just thinking of what you asked me about being molested."

"Well if anyone did molest you, I'd kill them," replied Michael.

At that point Selwyn felt a grasp on his swollen crotch, causing him to gasp.

"What's the matter?"

"Nothing. It's just the way you said you'd kill them. I didn't think that you were so threatening and violent."

Selwyn began to giggle as Greg's fingers found their way into the waistband of Selwyn's Speedo, extract his hard cock and then he felt a warm mouth encompass his length.

"What are you giggling for?" asked a concerned Michael. "It's not funny. I wouldn't want anyone molesting you. I feel for you too much."

"I know you do, Michael, so let's cut the crap and go for lunch. I'll tell you what, you go and start the car and I'll get dressed and meet you down stairs."

"You mean you're not dressed?"

"I've still got my Speedo on so I'd better put on some shorts or something. I'm sure you wouldn't want me walking about half naked in case I got molested."

"You mean you've been sitting here half naked and I didn't know. Come here," said Michael rising and beginning to move to Selwyn.

Selwyn immediately rose from the table without dislodging the tablecloth, and in doing so, Michael saw the erection that Selwyn had.

"And that? Where'd that come from?" asked Michael embracing Selwyn in his arms and feeling the hard-on press up against his stomach.

A giggle emanated from Selwyn as he tried to explain. "It's when I'm in your company that this sort of thing happens to me; now go and start the car before we do something we shouldn't be doing and we miss out on an early lunch."

Michael kissed Selwyn, gave Selwyn's crotch a gentle grope, grabbed his car keys and exited the apartment, leaving Selwyn to dress. Selwyn lifted the tablecloth, when he knew the coast was clear and found a grinning Greg still hiding there.

"What do you think you were doing?" asked Selwyn.

"Giving you a bit of pleasure. So I suppose you're off for lunch?"

"Yes and we've got to get you out of here without him seeing."

"I take it, 'him' is your boyfriend; but you know I really would like to see you again, if it's possible."

"No, you must go, in case he comes back to see what's keeping me."

"Sure, but you can't deny you enjoyed what was happening under the table."

"Stop talking and go before he comes back."

"Please can I see you again so I can finish what I started with you?"

"Fuck off before he walks through the door again," said Selwyn agitatedly. Selwyn then thought about the pleasure he'd been experiencing under the table. "OK, I might see you at the pool one of these days, now go," he said, getting desperate to get rid of his visitor, and actually ushering him out.

Selwyn quickly slipped on a tracksuit bottom, which he took from the clothing cupboard, and a pair of sandals, slammed the front door behind him and made his way down to the waiting car. As he and Michael drove off for lunch, he noticed Greg standing on the sidewalk watching them depart, smiling at him.

When they arrived at the designated restaurant, Selwyn slipped graciously from the front seat of the car and walked very dignified into the restaurant with Michael. There was nothing cheap about this restaurant; that was obvious not only from the décor but also from the prices on the menu. Selwyn liked being treated like a queen and Michael liked to spoil him. It was still early days in their relationship so Michael tended to spend a great deal on Selwyn, not that Selwyn objected.

The waiter arrived, bringing the menu and wine list to their table. Michael took charge of the ordering and ordered a bottle of Chardonnay to have with the fish, which he'd ordered, while Selwyn went for the spaghetti carbonara. After they had placed their order, Michael sat gazing into Selwyn's eyes like some love-sick puppy, telling him how much he loved him and how he didn't know how he'd survived before meeting Selwyn. Selwyn gazed back wondering whether Michael had an idea that there had been a man under their dining-room table just prior to their going to lunch.

"Are you happy with me, Selwyn?" asked the lovesick puppy.

"Of course! What do you think?"

"I really hope so, because I'm on cloud nine when I'm with you," continued Michael. "I really think that I've now met the right person for me with whom I could spend the rest of my life. All we need to do is find you a good job, and then everything will be in place."

"I have got my part-time job, you know."

"But you need something more reliable and steady," replied Michael, as the waiter arrived with the wine.

The wine was poured into Michael's glass, whereupon he sniffed it, swirled it, tasted it and then grinned at the waiter, who proceeded to pour some into Selwyn's glass.

"I'm very happy doing my three evenings a week stint," continued Selwyn, "after all I get a fair payment from the club and it's nice to see my old friends."

"That's what worries me," said Michael, with an air of concern in his voice. "It's not so much the friends I worry about, it's the others in the club who might try to pick you up or make passes at you."

"Love," said Selwyn, waving his arms about like a Dutch windmill in full flight on a gusty day, "You've got to trust me. I go there to do my show three nights a week, have a couple of drinks and then I'm on my way home. Really, most gays aren't interested in some drag queen standing up on stage cracking jokes and making a fool of herself."

"I do trust you, but I still think it would be better if you had a full-time day job so that we could spend our evenings together."

"But what happens when you have to go out at night with clients, then we can't spend our evenings together," rebutted Selwyn.

"Well that's the nature of my work."

"And doing a drag show is the nature of mine," insisted Selwyn.

Michael could see that he wasn't going to get Selwyn to change his mind, so instead he changed the subject.

"So tell me about your morning at the pool today?" enquired Michael. "Was it busy?"

"Just the usual tourists swimming in that ice cold water that makes your dick shrink to the size of a cocktail sausage, and some local geriatrics, going for their daily exercise. Other than that, it was very uneventful."

The food was delivered and placed dramatically in front of them. Selwyn looked at his pasta and then at Michael's fish; both dishes looked appetizing and there was no stopping Selwyn. He tucked into his pasta, slurping strands of spaghetti into his mouth much like a vacuum cleaner doing a blowjob on a carpet. Michael ate sedately and watched with enjoyment as Selwyn devoured everything on his plate as though this was the last supper.

When he'd completed his meal, Selwyn wiped his mouth very daintily with his starched, white napkin and said, "Shit, Michael that was good!"

Michael was exceedingly happy in Selwyn's company and they sat casually chatting and finishing off their bottle of wine together. It was during this time that Michael's mobile phone rang.

"Hello. Michael Bloomberg speaking. How may I help you? ... I've got a two-bedroom apartment in that area. If you're interested, I'll be able to take you there as I've got the key ... No, it's vacant at the moment ... Fine, then let's meet at our offices at 5 p.m if that suits you and I'll show you the place ... I'll see you at 5:00 then. Cheers."

Michael terminated the call and placed the phone on the table.

"I take it that means you're going to be late tonight?" stated Selwyn, looking a little depressed.

"Shouldn't be too long, unless he wants to put in an offer."

They finished their wine, paid the bill and Michael took Selwyn back to their apartment. As they rounded the corner to enter the parking garage of their building, Selwyn noticed Greg sitting on a bench across the road from their entrance to the building. Although their eyes didn't make contact, Selwyn thought it odd that this man had stayed waiting, but waiting for what? They parked the car and both young men went up to their apartment in the elevator. On entering the apartment, Selwyn sank onto the couch to watch some TV, while Michael, on the other hand, went into the bedroom for a short lie down on the bed.

"If I doze off to sleep, please wake me at about 4:00 so that I can freshen up before going on that appointment," shouted Michael from the bedroom.

Selwyn sat channel hopping on the TV for a while until he too decided to have a lie down and went to join Michael in the bedroom, but set his alarm clock for 4:00 before going to sleep.

At precisely 4:00, the shrill ringing of the alarm clock awoke both young men and Michael rose to freshen up, while Selwyn decided to start preparing dinner for them. Michael left for his appointment and Selwyn took a shower, laid the dining room table for their dinner and settled down to wait for Michael.

At 6:45, Michael arrived home from his appointment to be met by Selwyn and a hearty meal awaiting him. They sat down to eat together with Michael telling Selwyn about his evening's appointment.

"The guy I had to meet was very interesting," said Michael, helping himself to seconds of their meal.

"In what way?" enquired Selwyn, interested to know what Michael meant by 'interesting'.

"I might have a job for you, Selwyn."

"But I told you I had a job."

"I'm talking about a full-time job, not your evening escapades," replied Michael. "How would you like to work for a P.I. as his assistant?"

Selwyn burst out laughing at the suggestion.

"You have to be joking!"

"I'm not. We got to talking and it turned out that he was a Private Investigator with his own business and he was looking for an assistant, so I told him about you and he said he'd like to meet you and have a chat about it."

Selwyn had a look betwixt a glowing interest and one of anxiety.

"Is he young and good-looking?" joked Selwyn.

"I'm serious about this," answered Michael.

"So am I. Is he good-looking, because if he's not, then I'm not interested?"

"Yes, I suppose you could say he was good-looking," replied an unsure Michael, not knowing what Selwyn's ulterior motives might be.

"As good-looking as you?" continued Selwyn, grinning from ear to ear.

"Come on, be serious," barked Michael, now becoming a little agitated by Selwyn's lack of seriousness.

Selwyn tried to wipe the smirk from his face and once he had managed that, he spoke in a very serious tone to Michael.

"Very well. When do I meet this nameless man?"

"His name's Rob and you are to meet him tomorrow at his office at 11:30. I'll pick you up from here and take you to his place so that you can have a chat then I'll bring you back."

"Don't forget, I'm performing tomorrow night."

"What time?"

"I have to be there at 8 p.m. to get made-up," replied Selwyn, still maintaining his sincere approach.

"Don't worry; you'll be there with plenty of time to spare."

"Is he gay?" asked Selwyn, after a moment's pause.

"I don't know. I didn't ask him."

"But surely you could tell?"

"Do you mean was he as camp as you? No he wasn't, but I'll leave that for you to ask tomorrow, if you like."

Selwyn could sense that Michael was getting a little agitated by his humor and lack of sincerity about the work offer, so he decided to cool it and not upset his partner. The discussion about the job and Rob ended, and after an evening of little conversation, both men went off to bed.

Chapter 2

The following morning, both men were up early and Michael set off for work after having eaten his breakfast. Selwyn, on the other hand, wandered around the apartment as naked as the day he was born, tidying up and then showering. He went to his cupboard and scratched through his things to find something to wear for his interview. He pulled on a pair of white Calvin Klein briefs and then his blue jeans, which fitted snugly over his ass. He then pulled on a pale blue cotton shirt, tucked it into the jeans and then slipped on some shoes and socks. He admired himself in the full-length mirror in their bedroom cupboard. *Not bad looking*, he thought. He turned so that he could see his butt in the mirror.

"Hm! Pretty tight," he said, slapping it gently.

As he completed dressing, the telephone in their apartment rang. He knew it wouldn't be Michael, because he always rang on the mobile phone. He picked up the phone and answered.

"Hello, Michael's residence."

"Hello. Who's that?" enquired a female voice.

"Who wants to know," replied Selwyn.

"Who's speaking," came back the rather irritated reply.

"Selwyn!"

The tone of the voice at the other end of the line suddenly changed. It became less harsh and more genteel.

"And who are you Selwyn?"

"I'm a friend of Michael's."

"Oh, that's nice. I'm Michael's mother, Mrs. Bloomberg."

Selwyn was somewhat startled by this statement.

"Oh! Hello Mrs. Bloomberg. Can I help you?"

"Is Michael there?"

"I'm afraid not. He's already left for work."

"Oh. And what are you doing there Selwyn?"

"I live with Michael."

There was a stunned silence at the other end of the line.

"Hello Mrs. Bloomberg are you still there?"

Silence reigned.

"I… I didn't know that Michael had a friend staying with him. How long have you been there?"

"Two weeks," replied Selwyn confidently.

Stunned silence again.

"You said your name was Selwyn?"

"That's right."

"That's such a nice Jewish name. I suppose if my little Michael has met a nice Jewish boy, who am I to complain," came Mrs. Bloomberg's resigned reply.

Selwyn guffawed on hearing this. Jewish he was not, but he thought it inappropriate to inform Mrs Bloomberg of this as his shares might suddenly drop like a stock market in crisis.

"Yes, it is a nice Jewish name," remarked Selwyn.

"In that case I'm dying to meet you," continued Mrs. Bloomberg, now gushing with each compliment she made. "I hope that you're looking after my son."

"Oh yes, and he's looking after me as well."

"You sound such a nice young boy. What do you do, Selwyn?"

Now there was a stunned silence on Selwyn's side of the phone. He couldn't tell her he was a part-time drag artiste, nor could he say that he was unemployed.

"I'm in entertainment, Mrs Bloomberg, but I'm actually going for a job interview this morning for a full-time job."

"Entertainment?" questioned Mrs. Bloomberg, with an element of hesitancy in her voice.

"Yes."

"Oh." There was a pause and then, "Are you an actor?"

"You could say that," replied Selwyn.

"Oh." Once more a pause. "A dancer?"

"That too."

"Oh. And singing is that part of it as well?"

"Most definitely."

"You sound so talented. And how old are you, Selwyn?"

"Twenty-four, Mrs. Bloomberg."

"The same age as my Mikey. Oh that's lovely."

Selwyn was beginning to become edgy from the interrogation, so he tried to put an end to their conversation. "Mrs. Bloomberg, do you want me to give Michael a message when I see him?"

"No, no. I just wanted to find out how he was doing as I hadn't spoken to him for a couple of days, but it's funny he never said anything to me about you being there with him, but you boys will be boys."

Selwyn gave a nervous laugh.

"Well, I must be going, Mrs. Bloomberg. Stay well and look forward to speaking to you again."

"Bye Selwyn. Take care."

The phone went dead. Selwyn replaced the receiver and roared with laughter. He wondered what Mrs. Bloomberg would say if she could see him either in the flesh or in his drag outfits.

When Michael arrived at the apartment to collect Selwyn for his interview, Selwyn told him about his mother's phone call and how she loved his Jewish name.

"Oh shit!" exclaimed Michael.

"Why didn't you at least tell her that you had someone staying with you?" asked Selwyn, seeing Michael's predicament.

"I wasn't sure how she would take it. I'm still not entirely sure that she knows I'm gay. I've never told her."

Selwyn roared with laughter again.

"Sweety, she knows. Most mothers know these things. The only thing she doesn't know is that her future son-in-law might have a Jewish name, but he's a paler shade of brown and isn't Jewish. Do you think that'll put her off me?"

"Selwyn don't joke. This is serious."

"Who for? Your mother or for you?"

"For both of us."

"So if your mother doesn't like me, does that mean it's over for us?"

"Of course not. I'm not in a relationship with you to please my mother. I'm with you because I like you irrespective of whether she likes you or not."

"Only like!"

"Don't be silly. You know what I mean. Now come on, let's get going for your interview. That's more important than worrying about my mother."

They made their way down to the underground garage, got into the car and headed in the direction of Rob's office.

"When we get there, I'll introduce you to him and then I'll just wait out in the car until you've finished."

The building was a typically austere office block, brown brick with small glass windows. Selwyn and Michael parked the car and made their way up eight floors, exited the elevator and walked along a narrow corridor until they came to an office marked R.CLAYTON, Private Investigator. They knocked and went in. The office had a small reception area with a desk and a couple of easy chairs scattered around, but no one in attendance. Off this reception area was another door, which stood ajar and through which they could see another desk and two easy chairs. Behind the desk sat a large man who looked up on their entering.

"Hi there, Mike," shouted the man from his office.

He rose and came out into the reception area where he and Michael shook hands.

"Rob, let me introduce you to Selwyn. Selwyn this is Rob Clayton. Rob this is Selwyn Smith."

The two men shook hands and from the slightly pained expression on Selwyn's face, Michael knew that Rob's firm grip in his handshake had crunched a few of Selwyn's fingers.

"Pleased to meet you, Selwyn. Come through to my office and let's get acquainted," said Rob, leading the way and closing the door behind them, leaving Michael in the reception area. Michael decided not to wait down in the car, so made himself comfortable in an easy chair. He could hear the low voices coming from the main office.

Rob was a tall six foot five inches with broad shoulders and a trim waist. Although he was bald, it was not through a lack of vitamins to grow his hair, but rather he'd shaved his head. He looked like he might be in his late thirties or very early forties. His hands were large and strong, as Selwyn had felt, and his legs were sturdy like tree trunks. Selwyn's mind flashed to when he'd asked Michael if the guy was gay. He looked the man up and down and decided that perhaps he wasn't, but he liked what he saw; in fact liked what he saw very much. Rob, although had the appearance of a giant, had the manners and voice of a civilized, gentle man. He seemed mildly spoken and acutely interested in other people. At no time during their discussion did he talk about himself, but rather wanted to know everything about Selwyn.

"Where do you stay, Selwyn?" asked Rob, leaning back in his chair behind the large wooden desk.

Selwyn hesitated before answering because he didn't know whether Michael had said anything about them living together.

"I share an apartment with Michael," replied Selwyn.

"Nice guy, Mike," continued Rob. "How long have you been staying there?"

"Two weeks."

"Oh, so you've only recently met, then?"

Again Selwyn was a little hesitant in answering.

"Yes."

"And Mike tells me that you've been holding down a part-time job a couple of nights a week?"

Oh hell, thought Selwyn. *Please don't ask me what work I've been doing.* Selwyn hesitated once more, hoping that the question would go away, but it wouldn't.

"Yes I work at a club," was his reply.

"Barman?"

"No, I do the entertainment."

"That sounds great. I'd love to come and see you at the club," responded Rob.

"Oh I don't think you'd enjoy it, it's very low-key stuff you know."

"I like how modest you are," said Rob, now leaning across the desk, his strong arms folded. "Has Mike told you anything about my work?"

"No, nothing."

"Well as you obviously saw on the door. I'm a P.I. and as I'm sure you also saw when you entered the office, I have no-one in reception to deal with clients and phone calls, so I was thinking that perhaps you might be interested in taking on the job as my receptionist."

"Well I ..."

"... I'll pay well," interrupted Rob.

As he said this, Rob rose from behind the desk and walked around to Selwyn's side of the desk where he towered over the young man. Selwyn found himself looking directly at Rob's crotch level, and what a sight! He could see the emphatic bulge in the front of Rob's jeans and was almost tempted to stretch out a hand and gently touch the crown jewels to see if they were real, but he refrained.

"I'll take the job," stammered Selwyn as Rob extended a hand to him.

Once more Selwyn felt the strength in Rob's hand as they gripped each other's hand. Selwyn was lifted up out of his chair and rose to face his new boss.

"When can you start?" asked Rob, still holding firmly onto Selwyn's hand.

"Whenever you want," came the timid reply.

"How about the beginning of next week?"

"That's fine by me, Mr. Clayton."

"It's Rob. OK?"

"Yes, Rob, anything you say."

Rob opened the office door and the two men exited to the reception area.

"Well Mike, I've got myself an assistant. He's starting next Monday."

"That sounds great. Thanks Rob."

"Oh and Selwyn, I want to know when you're performing again. I want to see how good you are."

Michael wasn't sure what the reference was about, but looked quizzically at Selwyn, who raised his eyebrows.

"He's performing tonight," said Michael, innocently to which Selwyn glared back angrily.

"Unfortunately I can't make it tonight, but perhaps another night will do," said Rob, showing an element of disappointment in his face.

Selwyn smiled with relief and soon both young men had bade Rob goodbye and left the office.

Michael and Selwyn made their way down the elevator to their car.

"Why did you tell him about the show tonight?" asked Selwyn somewhat angrily.

"He did ask, so I told him. Why?"

"I don't want him to know that I'm a drag artiste."

"So are you saying that you don't think that he's gay then?"

"Definitely not. Not with that huge body of his and his crushing handshakes. Nice body though by the looks of it."

Selwyn wasn't about to say anything about the bulging crotch that he had viewed at eye level, but he was definitely impressed by what he had seen.

"So tell me what he said to you?" enquired Michael, as they reached the car.

"Oh just the usual. You know, what you are doing, where do you stay…"

"Did you tell him we lived together?"

"I just said we shared an apartment, but didn't say anything about being gay or in a relationship if that's what you mean."

"What else?"

"He spoke about salary and said that you'd told him that I was employed in a club."

"I didn't tell him what you did, though."

"Neither did I," replied Selwyn, "but he seems adamant that he wants to come and see me perform. Do you think he suspects something?"

"No, I don't think so."

Michael dropped Selwyn back at the apartment, said he'd see him at 5:00 and then sped back to his office. Selwyn got out of his clothes and slipped into a pair of shorts and T-shirt. It was lunchtime so he wondered if he should wander down to the pool or stay at the apartment. Before he had time to decide, he heard a soft rapping at the front door. When he opened it, there stood Greg.

"Is it safe for me to be here?" asked Greg.

Selwyn was taken aback by his presence and stood staring at the visitor, not quite sure whether to invite him in or not.

"Is your partner here?" enquired Greg, a little more persistent.

Selwyn was still undecided. If he let him in, he knew what was going to happen, and he didn't know whether he wanted it to happen or not.

"Greg, I don't think it's wise for you to come here because I never know when my partner is coming back, so it's not that safe."

"Please can't I come in just for a minute?"

"I don't think so, Greg."

Greg stood in the doorway, also in a pair of tight shorts, rubbing a hand across his gradually enlarging crotch. Selwyn's eyes obviously followed the hand and saw the crotch and felt his own beginning to swell. The two men stood staring at each other as their bulges steadily grew.

"You know you want this," said Greg, giving his swollen crotch a gentle squeeze.

Selwyn's eyes focused on the enlargement and instinctively he felt his own crotch. Yes he wanted it, but he knew that it was wrong. That damn devil was at it again. The devil and the angel sat on his shoulders.

Don't even think about it, said the angel.

Go for it, you want that big cock down your throat, commented the devil.

Selwyn could feel his mouth getting dry. He swallowed hard and automatically licked his lips. Greg saw this as a sign of acceptance and stepped forward. His hand reached out and took hold of Selwyn's burgeoning crotch, grasping it firmly. A gasp was emitted from Selwyn and he closed his eyes in pleasure. The two men stood in the doorway in ecstasy.

I warned you, said the angel. *You might regret this.*

Just think how you've wanted this. Stretch out and touch him. Take that hard cock and suck on it. You want to, taunted the devil.

Selwyn did as the little devil suggested and soon had Greg's cock firmly embedded in his mouth. Although they were in the public eye in the doorway, Selwyn was aware that the sooner he got this over with, the sooner Greg would leave. His mouth traversed the length of Greg's weapon, until he felt the gushing of warmth entering his throat. Selwyn swallowed and no sooner had Greg emptied his supply, than Selwyn rose to his feet, thanked Greg and slammed the front door shut.

Selwyn went and lay on the couch in the lounge luxuriating in the feeling that filled him. He was glad that he did it with Greg, and he enjoyed it, but he also felt guilty because he had gone behind Michael's back with someone else.

You need to tell Michael, said the angel.

What he doesn't see, he doesn't have to know about, said the little devil.

Slowly Selwyn dozed off into a happy sleep, only to be woken by Michael's lips tenderly caressing his.

"Hi there, it's time to get up and get ready for your show tonight, Sleeping Beauty."

Selwyn smiled up at Michael, and then the realization hit him. Should he tell Michael about Greg? If he did, they'd probably end up fighting, so it was better to keep quiet, which is what he chose.

Chapter 3

Selwyn arrived at the club with plenty of time to spare before his act began, so he and Michael decided to sit and have a drink together at the bar. Although it was quite early, the club was already filling up with a variety of clientele.

"Are you looking forward to your new job?" Michael asked Selwyn, taking a sip from his beer.

"I'm not entirely sure at the moment because I don't know what's expected of me."

"Didn't Rob explain everything to you?"

"He said I'd be receptionist and answer the telephones, but he didn't elaborate."

"Maybe you might find yourself being an undercover cop for him," joked Michael.

"You're joking, aren't you," replied Selwyn, suddenly looking a little tense at the thought of being a cop. "That could be dangerous, don't you think?"

"I suppose it could be, but I'm sure that you could handle it. You're a tough cookie!"

"Thanks for the vote of confidence, but I'm not sure that I want to go toting a gun all over the place."

Michael chuckled to himself, thinking what Selwyn might look like with a gun attached to his hip.

"What are you chuckling about?" enquired Selwyn.

"I had this picture in my mind of you with your six-shooter hanging from your hip while you strode out into the street to meet the bad guys and have a shoot-out."

"Michael, this is serious. You know I don't like guns."

"I'm sure you won't be carrying a gun at any time. In any case, Rob seems a large enough guy to take care of you if the two of you are staking out a situation."

When Michael said this, Selwyn immediately thought of his interview and finding himself at crotch level with Rob and admiring the large package that was presented to him. A shudder of excitement ran through him at the thought of working with this hunk of a man.

"Selwyn, where are you?" asked Michael, noticing the trance-like state his partner had gone into.

"Huh? Sorry, I was miles away."

"What were you thinking of?"

"Oh, nothing in particular. Hey listen," said Selwyn, suddenly changing the subject. "I think I'd better go and start getting ready. Are you going to wait here?"

"You don't think I'd miss one of your performances, do you?"

Selwyn scuttled off to his make-shift dressing room, which was actually one of the toilets, while Michael remained chatting to the barman behind the counter.

At precisely 9 p.m. the lights were dimmed, the music volume turned up and the MC stepped forward.

"Ladies and gentlemen, it gives me great pleasure to introduce to you the one, the only, the greatest…"

A drum roll sounded.

"The wonderful Princess Selena."

A spotlight hit the front of the small stage, which was situated at the far end of the bar, and a ravishingly beautiful Selwyn, with auburn shoulder-length wig and immaculate make up stepped into the light. The crowd cheered enthusiastically and applauded.

"Good evening my darlings. I would have said ladies and gentlemen, but I don't know if we have any gentlemen here tonight. It's so wonderful to see all your beautiful faces here tonight, and perhaps a little later, we might also see some of those beautiful bodies that some of you possess."

A giggle was emitted from Selwyn.

"Oh how naughty of me to say something like that, after all, my husband's in the audience tonight, so I'll have to behave myself, won't I?"

Loud cheers and laughter, echoed by a chorus of 'No!' reverberated around the club. Michael smiled at the suggestion.

Princess Selena opened her act with a rendition of Annie Lennox's *Sisters Are Doing It*, which got the crowd clapping and stomping their feet with enthusiasm. Michael watched proudly as Selwyn strutted his stuff on the tiny stage, belting out his song. What made Michael even more proud of Selwyn was that, unlike so many other drag artistes, he didn't lip-synch. Selwyn had a wonderful voice and had the ability to make it big on Broadway if he wanted to. At the end of the song, the crowd went wild, whistling and cheering and screaming for more. Selwyn obliged and went straight into his next number. While he was performing, Michael looked around the crowd to see the reactions of the many people. It was while he was scanning the faces of the crowd that he noticed someone in the doorway of the club. He sprang to his feet and waved to the person to get his attention. When their eyes met, the person made his way to the bar counter where Michael was standing.

"You made it," shouted Michael, over the noise of the singing and cheering.

"I had a cancellation so I decided to join you," said Rob, surveying the crowd. "This is quite some place, isn't it?"

"Is this the first time you've been here?" asked Michael.

"Yeh, but it seems quite a festive crowd."

Rob obviously stood out in the crowd, not only because of his height, but also because of his masculine build. Michael could see a few heads turning to look at Rob and give him admiring glances, so Michael decided to intervene.

"Stick close to me, Rob and you'll be fine," said Michael, sidling up next to Rob.

"Why, what do you mean?"

"If anyone asks, just say you're with me, that's all."

"OK," nodded Rob and focused on the singing.

When the second song was ended and the applause thundered, Rob turned to Michael and said, "Hey Mike, this chick's got quite a voice."

Michael smiled back at Rob, but wasn't sure whether he should tell him who the 'chick' in fact was, or whether he should let the show go on and then divulge it later.

As Selwyn's performance continued, he became a little more brazen with his jokes and often made references to people in the audience he could see. Although the spotlight hit him in the eyes most of the time, blinding him, occasionally Selwyn would try to block out the light and look around the audience. It was on one of these occasions that he suddenly spotted the tall Rob standing next to Michael. The smile on his face suddenly disappeared for a moment, but then just as suddenly reappeared. He continued his act until he reached his finale.

"Ladies and gentlemen, and others, for my last number I'm going to do a song from a group very close to my heart and many of yours as well – Queen..."

Shrieks and cheers greeted Selwyn's mention of the band.

"Ladies and gentlemen, *Killer Queen!*"

The music started and the crowd cheered. Selwyn seductively moved around the small stage and then decided to do something out of his usual routine. He stepped off the stage and ventured through the crowd. They loved this intimate contact they were receiving. Paths opened up allowing Selwyn to pass through. Slowly he made his way towards the bar counter where Michael and Rob were standing. As he reached them, he winked to Michael and then seductively ran a finger down the side of Rob's face. The gentle giant blushed. His smile increased ten-fold as Princess Selena stroked his face and then let a finger trickle across his manly chest. Michael stood aghast, but inwardly enjoying the situation. Princess Selena continued to flirt with Rob and at the end of the song, he gave Rob a gentle peck on the cheek and made his way back up on stage to take his bow. Everyone cheered, including Rob, who applauded wildly.

"What did you think of that?" asked Michael when Selwyn had disappeared backstage.

"That was bloody good."

"Now can I get you a drink? What would you like, Rob?"

"Beer, thanks Mike. Where's Selwyn?"

It was then that Michael realized that Rob hadn't recognized Selwyn as Princess Selena.

"I'm sure he won't be long and then he'll join us."

The DJ had put some music on and people were either dancing or getting themselves refills. Michael decided to change the conversation away from Selwyn's performance.

"Rob, I just want to thank you for offering Selwyn a job. I really appreciate it."

"You're welcome, buddy. I think he seems quite a decent sort of guy, if you know what I mean?"

Michael wasn't sure what Rob meant by 'decent sort of guy', but he wasn't about to question that.

"Yeh, I like him and get on well with him."

Michael noticed that although the dance floor was filled with men dancing with other men, Rob didn't react negatively. He thought that perhaps this giant of a man was open-minded or might even be gay. While they were talking, a couple of muscular guys sidled up close to Rob, but he chose to ignore them. One even offered to buy him a drink, but he politely refused, saying that he was still busy with his beer.

Out of the crowd appeared Selwyn wearing jeans and a T-shirt.

"Hi Rob, I thought you weren't going to make it tonight?"

"I was telling Mike here that I had a cancellation so I decided to pop along to watch your act. What time are you on?"

Michael and Selwyn glanced at each other. Rob obviously didn't know that Selwyn had flirted with him. Now they had a dilemma. Did they tell Rob it was Selwyn, or keep quiet about it? Selwyn took the initiative. He stroked Rob's face in the manner that Princess Selena did. Rob looked a little surprised at first and then the realization set in.

"Oh my God! Was that you, Selwyn?" asked Rob, surprise written across his face.

Selwyn nodded and both he and Michael waited for the reaction.

"In that case you were more than bloody good as I said to Mike, you were fucking awesome," said Rob, grabbing Selwyn and hugging him. "Why didn't you tell me?"

"We weren't sure how you'd take it, after all we haven't known you for that long, so we weren't sure," replied Michael.

"This is great! You do realize what this means?" asked Rob.

"No," both Selwyn and Michael responded.

"If I need you to go under cover, you're a master at it."

Michael and Selwyn merely stared at each other, knowing that they had earlier spoken about the possibility of Selwyn going under cover.

"How long have you been doing these sorts of show, Selwyn?"

"About two years now," replied the young man, now oozing charm at being asked about his talents.

"And where did you learn all these skills such as singing and dancing?"

Selwyn giggled.

"I've had singing lessons, but the dancing just comes naturally."

"And you, Mike; have you got any talents like this?"

"Afraid not," came the disappointing answer, "but I'm proud of Selwyn's talents. Rather have one in the household with talent than two competing against each other."

"Good point," remarked Rob. "I suppose it could lead to upheaval sometimes. But you say you two have only been together two weeks?"

"That's right," replied Michael.

"And where did you meet?"

"Right here. We both had a bit too much to drink one night and we got chatting after Selwyn's show and one thing led to another, and now we're staying together."

"That's great," said Rob, ordering another round of drinks for them.

The evening continued to be festive and the three men easily fell into conversation with one another. At midnight, Michael and Selwyn decided it was time to head home.

"We better be going, Rob, because I have to get up for work in the morning," said Michael, swigging the dregs of his beer.

"I suppose I'd also better be going," replied Rob. "Criminals to catch and lovers to uncover tomorrow."

"What do you mean by 'lovers to uncover'?" enquired Selwyn.

"Oh you'll get used to it when you come and work for me. Most of my business is spying of cheating husbands and wives. It might sound mundane, but sometimes it gets quite exciting, especially when I have to go off to other cities."

"What do you mean other cities?" asked Michael.

"Sorry, I should have told you. Some times I have to go off on trips and it might necessitate Selwyn accompanying me for undercover work."

Michael looked a little down on hearing this, but Selwyn had a twinkle in his eye at the thought of them going off together; they might even have to share a room together at some stage, but now he was getting carried away.

"Come on Selwyn, I think we must head home," said Michael, picking up his car keys and heading for the exit, followed closely by Selwyn and Rob.

Once they got outside, they said their farewells and headed in their different directions. Michael and Selwyn hardly spoke throughout their journey home. Michael found the idea of Selwyn going off to other cities without him, a little off-putting. When they arrived home, they checked the answering machine to find a message from Michael's mother: *Hello Michael, it's your mother. If you don't mind I'd like to drop round for Sunday lunch. I'm dying to meet Selwyn. Will midday do? Love you both. Bye.*

Michael and Selwyn stared at each other, without saying a word.

Michael stripped off and hopped into bed. When Selwyn climbed into bed alongside Michael, he cuddled up and whispered, "Are you upset about something, Michael?"

Michael never responded.

"If you don't want me to take the job, I won't, but it was your idea."

Michael turned to face Selwyn.

"It's just I never thought of you having to go away like Rob says you might have to."

"Are you jealous?" enquired Selwyn.

Michael didn't want to admit it, but yes, he did feel a little afraid that perhaps Rob and Selwyn might hit it off together, after all Rob was very good-looking and muscular, something he had noticed that Selwyn liked in a man.

"Listen you don't have to worry about anything," reassured Selwyn. "I'm sure nothing will happen because you saw Rob's behavior tonight, he never hit on any of those men and could quite easily have done so if he was gay. All we need to worry about is your mother coming for lunch."

"Oh shit, I've already forgotten about that," replied Michael, yawning. "But Sunday's still to come. Let's get some sleep."

The bedroom light was switched off and the two men cuddled up together.

A Boner Book

Chapter 4

Sunday morning arrived bright and sunny. Both men awoke and leapt from their bed, a spring in their step.

"Let's go to the pool this morning," suggested Michael. "I feel like getting some sun on this body of mine. How about it?"

"Sounds good to me. I'll make breakfast for us while you get our towels and things and then we can walk down there," suggested Selwyn.

Breakfast was hurriedly made, towels were collected, Speedos slipped on and the men were ready for their morning outing before Michael's mother arrived for lunch.

"By the way, what are you planning on giving your mother for lunch?" asked Selwyn, when he realized that nothing seemed to have been prepared.

"I was going to buy a takeaway on our way back from the pool."

"Oh that's fine then, but will your mother approve?"

"Approve of lunch or you?"

"Very funny! Both!"

"I promise you she'll like both."

"But she doesn't know that I'm African-American and not Jewish."

"So that'll be our surprise for her," remarked Michael, grinning from ear to ear at the idea of shocking his mother.

"Tell me Michael, had you ever been with an African-American guy before you met me?"

"In truth, no; but it's not that I had any disliking, it's just that I'd never met any African-American whom I was attracted to, until I met you."

"And you're happy being with me?" asked Selwyn, fluttering his eyelashes at Michael.

"I haven't kicked you out have I?"

"No. But you do love me, don't you?"

"I fuck you don't I?"

"Hell you can be facetious, but I know what you mean and I love you," Selwyn giggled.

"Right, get that cute ass of yours into action and let's head for the pool."

They made their way down to the pool, found a spot away from the water's edge, threw down their towels, stripped off their shorts and lay down. Michael oiled Selwyn's back as he wanted to tan that first, then Michael massaged tanning oil over his own buffed chest and trim stomach, then lay on his back to absorb the sun's rays.

After a while of tanning and getting hot, Michael said he was going to go for a swim.

"Are you coming for a swim?" he asked Selwyn, but his partner groaned that he was happy to doze in the glaring sun.

Michael trotted across the surrounding grass to the pool and sat on the edge, dangling his legs into the water. He felt the coolness of the water on his feet and legs and then jumped into the shallow end and stood there for a while allowing his body to adjust to the coolness of the refreshing water, then he dived under the surface and swam to the deep end. As he floated in the water, he noticed someone talking to Selwyn. The man was kneeling alongside his partner and they seemed to be engrossed in conversation. Michael remained floating for a while and then slowly swam back towards the shallow end. As he emerged from the water and walked up to their towels, his Speedo clung to his lithe, muscular body, revealing his well-endowed package tucked into the confines of the Lycra. When he reached his towel, the man stood up and introduced himself to Michael.

"Hi, I'm Greg," he said, extending his hand to Michael.

Michael took his hand, shook it and introduced himself, then lay down on his towel, facing the man who continued to stand.

"I was just talking to Selwyn here," said Greg, "and he was telling me that he and you were staying together."

Michael thought it an odd thing to say, but then maybe Selwyn knew this man from somewhere before Michael had met Selwyn. Michael also noticed how Greg seemed to focus his attention on looking directly at Michael's crotch. Selwyn, in the meantime, said very little. Michael could see that Greg had his towel with him so he obviously had come to the pool for a reason, so politely he asked Greg if he wanted to join them. Greg immediately accepted the invitation and settled his towel between Michael and Selwyn's towels. He pulled down his shorts and stepped out of them, revealing a set of sturdy legs and a good package encased in a lime green Speedo. He removed his shirt and Michael noticed the well-formed upper body and trim waist. Still Selwyn said nothing, except if a question was directed to him.

The three men lay next to each other, absorbing the sun's rays, and then Greg popped a question to Michael.

"I wonder if you wouldn't mind putting some tanning oil on my back for me, please."

Michael, being the gentleman that he was, obliged. Greg flipped over onto his stomach, smiled at Selwyn as he did so, and allowed Michael to pour some of the cool oil onto his shoulders. Michael gently massaged the oil into Greg's shoulders and then down his back until Michael's fingers ran along the waistband of Greg's Speedo. Greg could feel a tingling sensation in his groin as Michael massaged his back and Selwyn could see a slight enlargement in Michael's Speedo.

"I wonder if you wouldn't mind also doing my legs for me, please Michael?"

Michael gladly obliged. He sat up and knelt beside Greg and began rubbing the oil along Greg's thighs. His hands slid effortlessly up and down the length of Greg's legs, and all the while Selwyn watched with a slight smirk on his face.

Michael's fingers glided up the inside of Greg's thighs until they gently touched that part of Greg's Speedo which covered his balls. Michael felt a firmness and immediately his own groin awoke with pleasure, which Selwyn noticed. Michael tapped Greg's thighs gently as an indication that he was finished and then lay back down on his towel, his burgeoning erection outlined in his Speedo. Selwyn winked to Michael who blushed.

Greg lay resting his head on his arms, but facing Michael, watching his masseur's erection starting to diminish. Michael caught Greg watching him and the two men smiled to each other.

"I think I'm going for a swim," said Selwyn suddenly jumping up from his towel and heading to the water.

When he was out of earshot, Greg looked at Michael and whispered, "That package looks good."

Michael merely smiled, then Greg turned onto his side to face Michael. Michael could now clearly see that Greg also had an erection and the length was clearly outlined in his Speedo. Greg tried to adjust the lie of his engorged cock, but without success; it had a mind of its own.

"That also looks good," said Michael, eyeing the large package on display.

Seeing this was now Michael's undoing as his penis also took on a life of its own and strained to break free from the constraints of the tight Lycra. Soon Selwyn came running up over the hot ground and both Michael and Greg flipped onto their stomachs to hide their embarrassment.

"Michael, don't forget we have to get back for your mother's lunch," said Selwyn, knowing that Michael was somewhat embarrassed by his predicament.

"What's the time?" asked Michael.

Selwyn stretched into his shorts to retrieve his watch.

"Eleven forty," answered Selwyn. "I think we ought to be going, don't you?"

"I suppose so," replied a disappointed Michael.

"So soon," said Greg, raising his head to look at Michael.

"Afraid so," said Michael getting up from his towel with still some evidence of his predicament evident. "We're expecting my mother for lunch."

Selwyn also rose and started pulling on his shorts. As he did so, Greg rolled over for both of them to admire his torso and the erection, which he still had. Both Selwyn and Michael stared at the man between them and then looked at each other. As though reading each other's thoughts, Michael said, "Would you like to come round for a drink some time, Greg?"

"Thanks that would be great. When?"

"What about tonight," intervened Selwyn, "After your mother has gone home."

"Is that OK for you, Greg?" asked Michael.

"I'd like that very much. Can I bring anything with me?" asked Greg.

"Just yourself," smiled Selwyn. "Say about seven-thirty, if that's fine with you."

All agreed on the time and Michael gave Greg the address, although unbeknown to him, Greg already knew the address, then he and Selwyn set off home to prepare for mother.

"Seems quite a nice guy," said Michael as they walked back to the apartment. "Where did you know him from, Selwyn?"

Selwyn had to think quickly.

"Oh I met him a long time ago. Before I met you," replied the young man, without a blush.

"I would imagine that you've had a scene with him before; he looks your type."

Selwyn merely smiled and nodded. He wasn't about to incriminate himself too much, but at the same time he didn't want Greg to say that he'd been to the apartment before.

"What do you mean by 'my type'?"

"You know muscular, good-looking and with a big dick."

Selwyn laughed. "That sounds like your type also."

Michael joined in the laugh and the two of them set off to get some takeaway for lunch.

They bought chicken pieces, a green salad, a French loaf and some smoked salmon, especially for mother. Back at the apartment, they tidied up, set the table and waited for her arrival.

On the stroke of midday, there was a knock at the front door. Michael and Selwyn both steeled themselves for Mrs. Bloomberg's entrance.

Michael answered the door to reveal his elegantly dressed mother. She was on the short side, much shorter than Michael, with a broadly smiling face and impeccably styled hair. Her make-up was to perfection and her outfit would have been a hit at any synagogue. She almost looked as though she were going to a wedding or some such event. She hugged and kissed Michael in the doorway and then swept past him into the lounge where Selwyn was waiting.

"My boykie, where is this young man of yours?"

Mrs. Bloomberg entered the lounge and came face-to-face with Selwyn. She stopped in her tracks.

"Oh hello. Who are you?" she asked, an arched eyebrow suddenly forming.

"Mum, this is Selwyn," said Michael coming to the rescue.

There was a deathly silence as each person surveyed the other. Mother looked at Selwyn, then at Michael, as if to check that she was seeing the correct thing, then back to Selwyn. Both Michael and Selwyn knew what was going through Mrs. Bloomberg's mind.

Selwyn eventually broke the ice.

"May I get you something to drink, Mrs. Bloomberg? A cold drink, perhaps?"

Mother remained staring at Selwyn.

"Whiskey, Michael!"

"Certainly, Mrs. Bloomberg," said Selwyn, sailing into the kitchen to do the necessary chores.

"Michael, he's ..." she hissed.

"Yes, Mum, he's African-American."

"No, no, it's not that. He's not Jewish! I thought with a name like Selwyn you had met a nice Jewish boy, one that I could be proud of. What am I going to tell them at shul when they ask me about you and whether you've got a girlfriend or a wife?"

"Tell them the truth. Tell them that little Mikey is gay and that he's got a wonderful non-Jewish African-American lover. What better combination could you ask for?"

"Michael this could be the death of me."

"Rubbish, Mum. Selwyn is a wonderful human being. He's caring and loving and I love him. You chose Dad because you loved him, didn't you, and I've chosen Selwyn because I love him."

"Rubbish, that's different. Your father, God rest his soul, was a good Jewish man and he wasn't gay."

"Oh, so is that the problem? Is it because I'm gay, or is it because Selwyn's not Jewish?"

"Michael, don't confuse the issue.

"That's what I'm trying to find out. What is the issue?"

Mrs. Bloomberg sat down on an easy chair, heaving as though she were having a heart attack when Selwyn returned with the whiskey.

"There you go, Mrs. Bloomberg, one strong whiskey on the rocks."

Selwyn handed the glass to Mrs. Bloomberg. She stared at Selwyn before taking the glass, and then both he and Michael watched as she gulped the drink down in one fell swoop. She replaced the empty glass on a side table and then resumed her glaring at Michael and Selwyn.

"I think I need another drink, please."

Selwyn scuttled back into the kitchen to refill the whiskey glass, and then hurried back into the lounge, where he once again handed over the drink.

"Sit down you two," she said, pointing to both young men.

The two sat next to each other on the couch like two scolded children, while silence reigned. Mrs. Bloomberg retained her upright posture and constant stare until the whiskey found its way into the deep depths of her stomach, then she spoke; slowly and with directness.

"Selwyn, you sounded such a nice young boy on the phone…"

"…But Mrs. Bloomberg, you haven't spoken to me since you walked in, so how can you imply that I might have changed? I know I'm not what you expected, but when we spoke I never had a chance to explain to you. You assumed that I was Jewish because of my name, but at no time did I mislead you in any way. I love your son and he makes me happy, just as I hope I make him happy. I'd like to think that you are a free-thinking human with an open mind and that if two people love each other, what does it matter to others whether they are of the same sex or not? Whether they are the same faith or not? Would you rather have Michael unhappy for the rest of his life simply because you don't approve of the person he loves?"

Michael's hand slid across and took hold of Selwyn's. He had never heard Selwyn speak in such a manner before.

"Mum, I love Selwyn very dearly and I want to spend the rest of my life with him…"

"The rest of your life!" exclaimed Mrs. Bloomberg. "Your life has hardly started. How long have you known each other?"

"Two weeks," replied Michael hesitantly.

"Two weeks is not a lifetime, Michael," boomed his mother. "How do you know you want to spend the rest of your life with someone after only two weeks, hey? It's not like a trade-in that you can take back to the shop when it doesn't work any more or you're tired of it…"

"…But Mum, we do love each other and I know that we complement each other and I have no desire to trade in Selwyn as you might be thinking."

Mrs. Bloomberg remained silent, allowing her son's and Selwyn's words to sink in.

"Selwyn, I think I need another stiff drink," she commanded.

Selwyn hopped up and ran to the kitchen to refill Mrs. Bloomberg's glass.

Another whiskey on the rocks appeared but this time it never disappeared with such alacrity as the previous ones.

Again she stared at the two young men before continuing to speak. However, when she did speak, the tone of her voice had somewhat changed slightly.

"Michael, as long as you are happy, then it makes me happy. Are you sure that this is what you want?" asked his mother, still looking stern.

"Yes, Mum. I'm very, very happy with Selwyn and we both want to spend our lives together."

There was moment of dignified silence where one could have heard a pin drop.

"Then I give you my blessing," said a dignified Mrs. Bloomberg.

But before either boy could respond, she continued.

"Oh and Selwyn, if you are going to be part of the family, you'd better get used to calling me either Myra or Mum. I somehow think that if you're going to be Michael's partner for life, then I'd prefer Myra. Clear?"

Selwyn smiled for the first time since the outburst.

"Yes...Myra!"

"Now both of you come here and give me a hug."

Both young men stood up and went across to the middle-aged woman and hugged her sincerely.

"Now tell me Michael, what do you people do when you go into a relationship? I don't need to know all the sex bits, but do you have a wedding ceremony or what?"

"It's entirely up to the couple, Mum. These days a lot of couples are having civil marriages, but we haven't given any of that a thought."

"That's a relief, I was just a little perturbed that I might have to organize catering for some big function. Now tell me Selwyn, do you have parents and if so where do they live?"

"Both my parents are still alive, Mrs. ...sorry, Myra, and they live in Washington."

"I suppose that's all right. And what do they do?"

"Both are professors at the American University."

"Oh, very impressive," replied Mrs. Bloomberg. "Professors of what?"

"My Mum is a Professor of Mathematic and my Dad is a Professor of Social Anthropology."

"Most impressive," glowed Mrs. Bloomberg, now beaming more broadly. "And do you have any siblings?"

"I'm afraid I'm an only child."

"Mm! Just like Michael. You know I wanted another child but it was your father who wasn't in favor. He said one was enough."

"Well in a way, I'm glad," replied Michael.

"And tell me Selwyn, where did you go to school?"

"Mum, enough of this. Stop the interrogation. Are you ready for lunch?"

"About time. I thought we were never going to eat," replied his mother.

The table was set and all three settled down to a pleasant meal together. By the end of the meal, the atmosphere in the apartment was much more conducive and friendly; thanks not only to the meal, but also to the whiskeys that were consumed by Mrs. Bloomberg.

By the time Mrs. Bloomberg was ready to leave for home, she was in no state to drive, so Michael drove his mother's car, while Selwyn followed in Michael's car. When they deposited her at her home, she hugged and kissed both men profusely, thanking them for the wonderful day and making them promise to care for each other.

As Michael and Selwyn drove back home, they heaved sighs of relief because now their relationship was in the open as far as Michael's mother was concerned and she had approved of Michael's lover, so life could resume its course.

Chapter 5

At seven-thirty that evening, having cleared and washed their lunch dishes, Michael and Selwyn prepared for Greg's visit. They tidied up the apartment and prepared a few snacks. They had put out some beers and the whiskey that Michael's mother hadn't finished, but they had other liquor in the cupboard in case visitors wanted something else to drink.

Selwyn was a little anxious at Greg's visit as he wasn't able to forewarn him about saying anything of his previous visits, but he hoped to drop a word in his ear when he arrived.

At a quarter to eight, there was a knock at the front door.

"I'll get it," shouted Selwyn, hurrying to get the door. He opened it and there stood Greg in jeans and white T-shirt. Selwyn put a finger to his lips as if to indicate that Greg say nothing about their previous visits. Greg smiled, knowingly on seeing the signal.

"Come in Greg," said Selwyn, ushering Greg into the lounge where Michael was waiting.

"Hi Greg. Nice to see you again," said Michael shaking hands with him. He felt the tight grasp as Greg took his hand.

"Nice to see you as well," replied Greg, still staying attached to Michael's hand.

"Come in and sit down. What can we get you to drink?"

"What are you guys having?"

"I'm having a beer and I don't know what Selwyn's having."

"Beer for me as well," echoed Selwyn.

"That's fine by me too," said Greg getting comfortable on the couch.

Michael went out to the kitchen to get the drinks while Selwyn positioned himself alongside of Greg on the couch.

"Not a word about your previous visits," whispered Selwyn.

"Doesn't Michael know?" was the whispered reply.

"Heavens no!"

"Well maybe we'll have to suggest a three-some to him and see how he reacts," said Greg with a glint in his eyes.

Selwyn immediately beamed on hearing this suggestion. Although he genuinely loved Michael, Selwyn liked a lot – a lot of sex, that is.

Michael came back into the lounge with a tray carrying the beers and glasses. He handed them around and went and sat down in an easy chair facing Greg and Selwyn.

"So how did your lunch date with your mother go?"

Both Michael and Selwyn burst out laughing.

"Traumatic!" said Selwyn.

"No it wasn't that bad. It was a little tense to begin with, but after a couple of whiskeys, she loosened up and by the time we had to take her home, she was fine," related Michael.

"You mean you had to take her home?"

"Sure! Too much alcohol, but she eventually said she likes me," said Selwyn feeling proud of his achievement at winning over his future mother-in-law.

"Didn't you mother know about you two?"

"Unfortunately not and it was worse because she was under the impression that because Selwyn had what she considered was a nice Jewish name, her son had met up with a nice Jewish boy. You can imagine the reaction when she walked in and saw Selwyn."

All three laughed heartily.

"But finally, she accepted me," said Selwyn, finishing the story.

"What about your folks, Selwyn, do they know about you and Michael?"

"They know about me but I haven't told them about Michael yet, not that it should be a problem because they've always been of the opinion that you make your bed, so you must lie in it."

"I suppose that's a good way of looking at it," said Greg.

"And you, Greg, are you in any relationship or is there any one in your life?" asked Michael.

"Many years ago there was someone, but it only lasted a couple of months and then fizzled out, so I've spent the rest of my life on my own and I'm quite happy that way."

"But don't you get lonely?"

"Sure, sometimes, but then one doesn't have to be lonely. I go out and mix with friends if I feel lonely, or I'll go to a movie or a show."

"You haven't thought about settling down with someone again?" enquired Michael.

"I don't know. Maybe I'm too fussy about who I would want to spend my life with."

"But what type of person interests you?" asked Selwyn, sidling a little closer to Greg.

"I like friendly people. They must have a sense of humor. Obviously good-looking…"

"…Obviously!" echoed Selwyn.

"I don't know … people like yourselves. Do you know what I mean?"

"Oh yes, we know what you mean," replied Selwyn continuing his light-hearted banter. "Guys like us who are hunky, brilliant conversationalists, witty, wonderful in bed and generally just great people."

"You're not talking about yourself, are you?" quipped Michael.

"Of course I am, and you, or weren't you aware that you had all those qualities as well

Michael merely chuckled to himself.

"Wow, you two sound like the ideal couple. Yes that's exactly what I would be looking for," joked Greg, slapping Selwyn on the thigh.

"Do you know what Selwyn's type is, Greg?"

"Michael, keep that mouth of yours shut or I'll spill the beans on you."

"He likes tall, well-built young men. It doesn't matter whether they're blond or not and they must have big dicks – the bigger the better."

Selwyn groaned in desperation.

"You are so tired. Of course I'm not like that. I like my men like I like my coffee, strong and pleasant tasting," remonstrated Selwyn.

"Well, there you go, I said well-built, but you used the word strong, so I was right."

Greg sat fascinated by the banter between Michael and Selwyn, not wanting to interrupt.

"All right, Selwyn tell me this: would you take Greg to bed if you had the chance?"

41

Selwyn's grin disappeared slightly. How was he to answer this question? He had wanted to do just that, but he wasn't sure how Michael would react if he did.

"Come on, I'm waiting for your answer. He's good-looking, strong and I'm sure he's got a big dick, so would you?"

Greg blushed when he heard Michael's description of him.

Selwyn turned to Greg and smiling, said, "Yes, definitely. Would you?" he quickly added.

It was Michael's turn to face Greg. He looked at the visitor and remembered their interaction at the pool. He could feel a rousing in his groin as he reminisced their lying together on the grass.

"Yes, I would too."

"Excuse me, but may I say something now?" intervened Greg.

"Sure," answered Michael.

"If I could, I would take you both to bed with me. So there, now you know."

Everyone remained silent but content, awkward smiles on all faces. Now what?

Michael and Selwyn glanced at each other, then Selwyn rose and said abruptly, "Michael can I see you in the kitchen please?"

Michael followed his partner to the kitchen where Selwyn stood waiting.

"Did I hear this whole conversation properly?" asked Selwyn. "Did we both say we'd like to take Greg to bed and did he say he wanted to go to bed with us?"

"You heard the same as I did, so now what?"

"I don't know," replied Selwyn, hesitantly, and then added more confidently, "I'm game if you are, Michael."

"The three of us, is that what you're suggesting?"

"Well, unless you've got a couple of extras in mind, sure, the three of us. It might be good fun."

Michael looked deep into Selwyn's eyes to confirm his partner's willingness.

"OK!" Let's ask Greg."

Together the two men marched back into the lounge to confront Greg, but the lounge was empty.

"Where's he gone?" asked Selwyn, more than a little surprised.

"Maybe he's in the bathroom."

"No, the door's open and no one's in there. Do you think he snuck out when we were in the kitchen?"

Just then a voice came from their bedroom.

"I'm in here guys."

Michael and Selwyn padded through to the bedroom to find a naked Greg casually draped across their bed.

"I thought you two were never coming back so I got tired of waiting."

Initially Selwyn and Michael were speechless, but before too much thought could take place, clothes disappeared quicker than a flash of lightning on a stormy night and Selwyn and Michael were on the bed on either side of Greg, caressing his firm, strong body and giving each other enormous pleasure.

While Selwyn's mouth searched Greg's, Michael slid between Gregg's thighs and took Greg's hard cock deep into his mouth, salivating along its length. His tongue caressed the underside length, licking it until his lips encircled the cut head of Gregg's broad cock.

Both Michael and Selwyn kissed the full length of Greg's body, licking and sucking at various erogenous areas until Selwyn unwrapped a condom on Greg's throbbing cock, lubricated his tight ass and slowly sank down onto Greg's hard cock.

"Aargh fuck!" exclaimed Greg as he felt the tightness of Selwyn's ass encircling his hard muscle.

Selwyn began a slow rhythmic movement as he rode Greg's bargepole and Greg's mouth took Michael's equally long, thick cock into its warmness.

Soon positions were changing again until each of the young men were satisfied and had been pleasured by the others.

In the early hours of the following morning, Greg emerged from under the covers of the bed, dressed and left, leaving Michael and Selwyn both satisfied and happy.

When they awoke in the morning, Michael went out to the bathroom and then into the kitchen to make some coffee. As he opened the curtains in the lounge, his eyes fell on a piece of paper lying on the couch. He picked it up and casually read the note: *Michael and Selwyn, thanks so much for last night. It was truly great sharing the evening with you both. Any time you feel like sharing again, call me on 678-2546. Cheers, Greg.*

Michael wandered back into the bedroom where Selwyn was still dozing in bed.

"There's a note from Greg. He must have left during the night."

Selwyn opened his eyes and took the note from Michael. He read it slowly then handed it back.

"Ah, that was sweet of him. You liked him didn't you, Michael."

"Yes, I actually did. He seems a decent sort of guy. I know you sure liked him."

Selwyn giggled. "Did it show?"

"Did it show! You were crying for more and you didn't want it from me," replied a scornful Michael.

"Well so would you if you were getting something that big."

"You're an unbelievable size queen."

"I can't help it if I like a lot."

"Come on tart, it's time you got up as you've got to get to work today. You're no longer going to enjoy the luxuries of being a housewife. From now on you're earning a living."

Chapter 6

Michael drove Selwyn to work, dropped him outside of Rob's building, said goodbye and set off to his office. Selwyn made his way up to the eighth floor and to Rob's office. He knocked on the door and went in.

"Is that you, Selwyn?" came Rob's voice from his office.

"Yes, Rob."

"Come through and have some coffee; I've just made some."

Selwyn made his way through to Rob's office and found his boss sitting casually in his chair, sipping his coffee.

"Welcome to the captivating world of intrigue, crime and desperate housewives."

Selwyn poured himself a cup of coffee and sat down across the desk from Rob.

"Basically for the first few days, I want you to answer the phone, take messages and keep me informed on progress of the cases that I'm working on, OK?"

"No problem."

"An important aspect of this type of job is confidentiality. What you see and hear must remain between us. The reason I want this is so that innocent people aren't affected by our findings and investigations. As I explained to you, there might be times when we have to go out of town and there might be times when you'll have to work late. Is that OK with you?"

"Fine by me."

"And is Mike happy with you working here and possibly going out of town?"

"He seemed a little upset when I told him about going to other cities, but if it's part of the job, then I have to do it," answered Selwyn, draining the last drops of coffee from his cup.

"Right let me get you up to date with what's happening here," said Rob clearing a space on his cluttered desk and pulling out a file and opening it. "Selwyn, a Mrs. Marriner is coming in this morning to see me. When she arrives I want you to usher her straight in to my office and stay so that you can take notes while I talk to her, right?"

"Sure boss! In the meantime, I'll go and tidy my desk."

Selwyn left Rob's office and started to tidy his desk in the reception area. Most of the pieces of scrappy paper he threw into a bin while the files that were scattered around the reception area, he placed in a filing cabinet that was like the focal point of the reception area. Although he didn't have access to any flowers, Selwyn decided that he wanted to brighten up the reception area and make it a more welcoming place, especially for people coming in to discuss their legal problems.

At 10:00, Mrs Marriner waltzed in through the front door and announced herself to Selwyn.

"Dear boy, I have an appointment with Mr. Clayton," said Mrs. Marriner, flinging herself into one of the two easy chairs in the reception area.

Selwyn buzzed and told Rob that Mrs. Marriner had arrived, but he replied that he wasn't quite ready for her yet.

She was a woman of about mid-fifties, elegantly attired, with clearly dyed hair, slightly over made-up and loud. Selwyn sat behind his desk and watched her. His eyes went down to her hands. *Ah ha!* he thought. *With those wrinkled hands and that taut face, she's obviously had a face-lift!*

"What are you looking at, young man?" came the stern voice and cold stare.

Selwyn smiled enigmatically at the lady.

"I was just admiring your outfit, Mrs. Marriner. Very good taste."

"Thank you young man," she beamed.

Just then Rob buzzed Selwyn and told him he could bring Mrs. Marriner through to his office. Both Selwyn and the client rose and went through to the other office.

"Mr. Clayton, how do you do. I must say that you have a very charming young man as your front line of defense," said Mrs. Marriner turning to me as she spoke.

"Thank you Mrs. Marriner. Yes he his very charming," replied Rob, smiling at both her and Selwyn. "Selwyn would you mind giving Mrs. Marriner a seat and then taking notes for me?"

"Certainly sir."

Mrs. Marriner sat directly across the desk from Rob while Selwyn placed his chair in a corner and readied himself with pad and pen.

"Now, what can I do for you, Mrs. Marriner? You briefly mentioned a few things to me over the phone, but would you like to give me more details?"

"It's my husband!"

"What about him?"

"I think he's having an affair," said the now stern lady.

"And what makes you think that?"

"A woman's intuition, my dear man. That is something we have that you men don't seem to have acquired."

"Quite right," said the obliging Rob, "but do you have any evidence?"

She hesitated.

"Well, for starters," she said, "we don't have sex any more and when I do feel like it, he keeps telling me he's got a headache. Headache, my foot!"

Rob and Selwyn threw a glance to each other and stifled a laugh.

"Yes I know that people always say that's the woman's usual excuse for not wanting sex, but he never seems to want it," continued Mrs. Marriner.

"But, madam, that's insufficient evidence to warrant an investigation on your husband."

"Well, if he's not having sex with me, then he must be having it with someone else," remonstrated the woman, "and I want to know who that person is. It has to be one of those floozies at the gym."

"Oh, does your husband go to a gym?" enquired Rob.

"Yes, four days a week he's down at our local gym, doing what I don't know because he doesn't have a Mr. Universe body to show for it."

Selwyn wrote notes furiously as the middle-aged lady rambled on.

"I'll tell you what I'll do, Mrs.Marriner, I'll stake out the gym and see what he does when he goes there and then I'll be able to give you some feedback when we actually have concrete evidence."

"That sounds reasonable, but when will you start?"

"Immediately. Either my assistant here or I will be at the gym first thing tomorrow morning. You said your husband always went there between eight and nine in the mornings?"

"Yes. He's tall, slim with dark hair, and here, I have a photo of him for you," said Mrs. Marriner, handing Rob a small photo across the desk.

Rob took the photo, looked at it then looked at Mrs. Marriner.

"Mrs. Marriner, how old is your husband?"

"Twenty-nine," she replied confidently.

Selwyn gulped on hearing this and once more stifled a giggle.

"Mrs. Marriner, leave it to me. I'll get to the bottom of this, but before I do, I need to discuss my fees with you, so Selwyn, would you mind excusing us for a moment, please."

Selwyn rose from his seat in the corner and exited the office, closing the door behind him. When he reached his desk, a broad smile covered his face as he thought of this middle-aged woman and her toy-boy husband.

After a moment, the inter-leading door between the two offices opened and Rob and Mrs. Marriner emerged. She gushed at Selwyn and shook hands with Rob before leaving. Both Rob and Selwyn waited until they knew that she was well out of earshot, then both burst out laughing.

"Now you know what I have to put up with sometimes, Selwyn."

"She obviously has money to have a toy-boy for a husband," said Selwyn, giggling.

"Right, we need to get down to business. Tomorrow, I'm going to come in late as I'll stake out the gym and see what I can find out and then perhaps on the other mornings, you can stake out the place, Selwyn."

"Do you think I look the type to fit into a gym environment? Michael's more of the gym type, not me."

"But you look as though you have a trim body, so I'm sure you'd look the part, but don't worry about it now. First we have to establish contact with the subject."

Rob went back into his office while Selwyn busied himself at his desk. Just then the telephone rang on Selwyn's desk.

"Rob Clayton Private Investigator, how may we help you?"

"Ooh, very formal!" came the voice.

"Hi Michael, how's it?" said Selwyn recognizing his partner's voice.

"I just wanted to know whether you'd settled in and how things were going."

"Great. We've already had our first customer today; a woman in search of her philandering toy-boy husband who apparently is having an affair with someone at his gym."

"And how old is she?"

"I reckon in her mid-fifties, and he's in his twenties."

Both men roared with laughter.

"But do you think you'll be happy there?" asked Michael.

"I think so, and Rob seems quite nice and friendly. He's going to be late tomorrow because he's going to stake out the gym where the toy-boy husband goes and see what happens there, then he said I might have to go and check it out on the other days this week."

"You in a gym!" exclaimed Michael. "You're having me on."

"Don't laugh, this is serious. There's nothing wrong with my body."

"No you're right about that, but you hate gyms and all that 'unnecessary lifting of heavy objects' as you put it."

"Well you never know. I might become the next Mr. Universe."

"You wish, but if you did, I'd have to lock you up so that no one else could get at you for your body. But seriously, why I phoned was to ask you if you were working at the club tonight, because if you weren't, I was going to suggest we go to movies."

"That sounds like a good idea. I'm only working on Wednesday, Friday and Saturday this week, so I'll be free tonight."

"Do you want me to fetch you from work or are you going to get a cab home?"

"Do you mind fetching me, then if you want to we can go and have something to eat and go straight to movies from there."

"Sounds fine to me. What time should I fetch you, Selwyn?"

"Just hang on a second. Rob," shouted Selwyn through to the other office, "I've got Michael on the line and he wants to know what time we finish work so that he can fetch me."

"You can go off at 4:30 if you like," came the reply.

"Did you hear that, Michael, four-thirty?"

"Right, I'll be waiting downstairs for you."

"See you later then. Cheers."

The conversation ended and Selwyn busied himself with more filing and tidying up.

At lunchtime, Rob asked Selwyn to go out and get something for them to eat. When Selwyn returned the two men sat in Rob's office eating their lunch and chatting.

"While you were out, I got a call from a guy who needs us to investigate his boyfriend. The only problem is the boyfriend seems to be in Florida," said Rob.

"How come he's here and the boyfriend's in Florida?"

"Apparently the boyfriend up and left him."

"But isn't that just a lover's tiff? Plenty of people break up their relationships and go off somewhere else."

"Sure, but this seems different."

"How so?"

"The boyfriend's apparently taken his credit cards, the car and he seems to be milking the guy's bank account."

"But isn't that a job for the police? You know, fraud and all that? What does he want us to do?" asked Selwyn.

"He just said that he didn't want to go to the police about it, that's all."

"So what are we going to do?"

"He's coming in tomorrow morning and as I'm going to be at the gym, you'll have to deal with him. This will be your first solo case. How about that?"

Selwyn sat agog.

"What if I make a mess of it?"

"You won't. I trust you and I'm sure it won't be difficult. In any case, we can't be expected to just drop everything and head off to Miami. We'll have to do some planning before we decide to head south."

"Does he know that you're not going to be here tomorrow?"

"Yes. I've already explained the set up to him. His name is Gary Jackson and he should be here by 9:00. Just note everything and ask plenty of questions to get as much information as possible."

Rob had opened a file for Gary Jackson and gave it to Selwyn for the following morning's meeting. At 3:00 that afternoon, Rob shouted through to Selwyn.

"Selwyn, if you want to phone Michael and tell him to fetch you now, you can. I don't think we're going to get any business this afternoon, so I thought we'd close early."

This pleased Selwyn who immediately contacted Michael and was soon waiting out on the street for his partner to arrive. That evening, they had a pleasant dinner together and went to movies, then shuffled home for a nightcap and to chat about Selwyn's new job.

Selwyn told Michael about his appointment the following morning and how nervous he was about conducting the interview, but Michael calmed him and reassured him of his abilities.

"You'll be fine, just do as Rob suggested and everything will be OK."

That night Selwyn battled to fall asleep as his mind was thinking about the following day's events, but with a cuddle from Michael, the two men soon dozed off to sleep.

A Boner Book

Chapter 7

Bright and early the following day, Selwyn was at the office. In fact he had caught a cab to get there early as Michael never had any appointments until mid-morning, so he'd decided to sleep in. He unlocked the office and decided that he'd conduct the interview with Gary Jackson in Rob's office, so he went into Rob's section and 'snooped' around.

Rob seemed a bit of an enigma to Selwyn. Sure he was friendly and charming, but other than that Selwyn knew nothing about the man, and Michael hadn't said very much about Rob, because he too knew very little about him. Selwyn sat behind Rob's desk and pulled open the top left-hand drawer. Inside he saw some papers, a calculator, Rob's diary and some pens and pencils. Selwyn surreptitiously removed the diary and opened it. On the inside cover was Rob's name and his personal details.

"So the guy's actually forty," said Selwyn, muttering to himself. Other than his date of birth, there was nothing incriminating in the diary.

Selwyn opened the top right-hand drawer, which contained more papers through which he ruffled. As he did so, he noticed a small photo between the papers. He took it out and looked at the person. It was a photo of a young man, probably early twenties or late teens, with slightly long fair hair and a smiling open face.

"I wonder if this is his son," muttered Selwyn once more, "but I don't even know if he's married. I've never heard him mention marriage or a wife. God! Maybe it's a boyfriend!"

Selwyn looked closely at the picture and then returned it to its hiding place and closed the drawer. While Selwyn was sitting behind Rob's desk, he heard the office front door open, so he went out to see who it might be.

In the reception area stood a blond guy of average build and with a pained expression on his face.

"Morning, can I help you?" asked Selwyn.

"I'm sorry, I'm early," replied the young man.

"Oh, are you Mr. Jackson?" enquired Selwyn, extending his hand. "I'm Selwyn."

"Yes," came the slightly reticent reply.

"Please come through into this office," said Selwyn, leading the way. "Have a seat."

Gary Jackson sat in one of the easy chairs, while Selwyn positioned himself in Rob's chair.

"Rob warned me of your visit. Would you like some tea or coffee?'

"Er... no thanks," replied Gary Jackson, fidgeting slightly.

"Mr. Jackson, you can relax here, there's nothing to worry about here with us."

"Thanks ... but please call me Gary."

"Very well Gary, as I said, I'm Selwyn. I always think its better to dispense with formality and easier to be on first name terms, don't you?"

"Oh... yes," stammered Gary.

"Now what can we do for you?"

"This is embarrassing."

"Trust me, nothing embarrasses us here. Just be perfectly honest and open with us and everything should go fine."

"Thanks. It's my ... my..."

"Yes?"

"My... boyfriend," continued Gary, almost showing what a weight had been lifted from his shoulders having said the word 'boyfriend'.

"What about your boyfriend, Gary?"

"He's left me for another guy, I think."

"Unfortunately these things do happen in the best of relationships, but what actually is the problem?"

"He seems to have gone to Miami and taken my credit cards with him and is milking me dry financially. Not only that, but he's taken my car as well."

"You never gave him any of these things and none were registered in his name?"

"No."

"So what exactly do you want us to do?"

"I want you to find him for me and put a stop to his fraud."

"Gary, do you have a photo of him for us?"

He dug into his jacket pocket and produced a color photo, which he handed to Selwyn.

"Him, quite good-looking, if I may say, and how old is he?"

"Twenty-two."

Selwyn looked up at Gary and decided that Gary couldn't have been much older himself, probably even younger.

"Does he have a name?"

"Byron Browning."

"And what does Byron Browning usually do for a living?"

Gary hung his head.

"I think Byron feeds off wealthy guys."

"Oh, I see. I take it that is what he was doing with you?"

"Not at first, but then after some time I noticed that he was more interested in my money than in me."

"Please don't think me rude, but I need to get as much information as possible, but how wealthy are you? What sort of amount of money was he taking from you?"

"My father owns an IT company, so, yes you could say we're well off."

"I see. Now when did Byron disappear?"

"A week ago."

"And what makes you think he's in Miami?"

"That's where the withdrawals are constantly being made. Whenever he makes a withdrawal or uses my credit card, it registers that the transaction took place in and around Miami."

By this time, Selwyn had noticed that Gary had become more relaxed and was willing to discuss his relationship with Byron, quite openly.

"You said that when Byron first moved in with you, things were fine, but then things changed. Did you find that his interest in you physically, changed?"

"Do you mean did we have regular sex? Our sex life diminished quite radically. I was also unsure whether he was going out and looking for guys behind my back."

"Do you have any evidence that he might have been doing that?" enquired Selwyn.

"No, but I just have this idea that he was probably doing something like that. What other reason could there be?"

Selwyn looked at Gary and thought the young man might be right. Gary was good-looking and most men would want to have a relationship with someone as good-looking as him, so for Byron to stop having sex might very well mean that someone else had come into Byron's life.

"Gary, leave it to us and we'll see what we can dig up for you. If we find him, do you want him back in your life?"

"No. I just want this theft of my possessions to be ended."

"But tell me, haven't you thought of canceling your credit cards?"

Gary hesitated before answering.

"It's more than that, Selwyn, he's taken other things that belong to me."

"Such as?"

"Bonds, jewelry and property ..."

"...What do you mean property?"

"I bought a house in both our names and he's now trying to sell it without me knowing."

"He can't do that!"

"I know, but if it means forging my signature to do it, he'll do anything. Please can you help me?" pleaded Gary.

"Listen, we'll do what we can. Give me all your details and those of Byron's and when my boss comes in this morning I'll pass it on to him and we'll see what we can do."

"Thanks, Selwyn. You seem such an understanding person and I respect that. You don't think that you could handle the case for me."

"Gary, between the boss and me, we'll make a plan and one of us will take charge of the case, but he's also very understanding, so you don't have to worry."

Selwyn then took down all the details and once again asked Gary if he'd now like a cup of tea or coffee.

"Thanks, Selwyn that would be nice. Coffee if you don't mind."

"The kettle's in the other office so do you want to come with me and we can have it there."

Both men went through to the reception area where Selwyn made coffee for them and then they made themselves comfortable again and sat chatting about things in general.

"You know, Selwyn, I don't like to say this, but your face seems familiar. Have we met somewhere before?"

"Not that I know or remember," replied Selwyn.

"Do you ever go to any bars or clubs? It might have been there."

Selwyn wasn't about to reveal his secrets of the night, so he merely shrugged and remarked, "perhaps."

As they were sitting having their coffee, Rob came into the office.

"Hi Rob, this is Gary Jackson, my appointment from this morning."

"Oh, Hi! I hope that Selwyn's been looking after you?"

"Very nicely thanks. Well I suppose I'd better be going," said Gary placing his cup on Selwyn's desk.

The two young men shook hands and Gary made his departure. Selwyn then went into Rob's office to find out how his boss had done at the gym.

"Did you have any luck this morning, Rob?"

"Oh yes, and I can tell you that the photo Mrs. Marriner gave us, doesn't do her toy-boy husband any justice."

"What do you mean?"

"He's a hunk and far better looking than in the photo. I actually can't imagine how someone as good-looking as that could have hitched up with a woman like her, but then I suppose money does strange things to people."

"And did you see him having an affair with any dusty maiden?"

"No."

"Nothing exciting?"

"Oh yes!"

"Well, don't keep me in suspense, what?"

"I saw how he spent quite some time with another guy. Of course they could have been doing weights together, but I found it odd that he made no advances towards any of the female members, which Mrs. Marriner seems to think."

"So do you think nothing is actually going on and that it's all a figment of her vivid imagination?"

"It could very well be her imagination, but we'll have to look into this more and see what happens, but now tell me about Mr. Jackson."

Selwyn related all the information on Mr. Jackson to Rob, who sat listening attentively. When Selwyn had finished explaining everything, Rob turned to him and asked, "What do you think is going on in their relationship?"

"I think that Gary Jackson is genuine in his concern."

"Do you think it warrants a trip to Miami?"

Selwyn didn't respond. Yes, he felt he could do with a 'holiday' in Miami, but he also didn't want to go there on his own. Rob sensed what was going through Selwyn's mind.

"If we have to go to Miami, would Michael object?"

"We?"

"Yes, you and me."

Selwyn was flummoxed because he wasn't thinking of himself and Rob, but rather of he and Michael.

"Or did you want to go on your own?" asked Rob.

"No, no, not at all. I'm sure it would be fine for us to go, if that's what you want."

"Look, let's not worry about that yet. I'll make some calls to Miami and see where that gets us then we can take it from there, OK?"

"Sure," replied a relieved Selwyn.

Selwyn went back to his desk and Rob to his. As the two men sat in separate rooms working, Selwyn heard Rob call him, so he got up and went into his boss's office.

"Selwyn, were you looking for something while I was out?"

Selwyn blushed because he knew that he'd been caught out snooping in Rob's drawers, but how?

"I was just looking for some paper," said Selwyn, sounding a little unbelievable.

"And did you find what you were looking for?"

"Thanks."

At that, Rob ended the conversation and Selwyn sidled back to his desk, embarrassed.

When it was time to knock off and go home, Selwyn knocked on Rob's office door. Something had bothered him throughout the day and his conscience was now pricking him.

"Rob can I have a word?"

Rob looked up and Selwyn felt intimidated by the look he received.

"What is it?"

"Rob, I saw a photo in your drawer…"

"…yes?"

"A photo of a young guy…"

"…yes?"

"I was just wondering…"

"…yes?"

"Is he a friend?"

Rob smiled slightly.

"Selwyn if you must know, he's my son."

Selwyn's face changed first from surprise then to relief.

"I used to be married and I had a son, but my wife and I divorced many years ago. Why, who did you think it was?"

"I wasn't sure. And where is your son now?"

"He's in California, working there, but we try to see each other as often as possible."

Rob could see the relief in Selwyn's face, but added: "Selwyn, anytime you want to know anything, ask and leave the snooping to the Private Investigator!"

"I'm sorry Rob. It won't happen again."

"Now go home. Haven't you got a performance one of these nights?"

"Wednesday," replied Selwyn.

"Maybe I'd better come and watch it from start to finish this time, instead of coming in half way through."

Selwyn blushed as he left Rob's office and made his way home. When he got home he told Michael of the day's events, including the photo he had found of Rob's son and the possibility of him and his boss having to go to Miami.

"I was hoping that I might be able to take you to Miami," said Selwyn, "but it looks like it'll be Rob and me, if we have to go."

"Selwyn, you must understand, it's part of your job. What would I do there while you were working?"

"Have a holiday."

"No, it makes absolute sense for Rob to take you, but as you said, it might not happen. But tell me, is his son as good-looking as his father?"

"Definitely, but he also said that he wanted to come and see my show from beginning to end."

"That would be nice for you, so why don't you invite him to Friday or Saturday's performance. Maybe we could invite him round for drinks if you like," said Michael.

"That's actually a nice gesture," replied Selwyn.

But Friday and Saturday's performances had to be cancelled because Rob and Selwyn had to fly to Miami, while Michael was roped in to staking out the gym for Mrs. Marriner's toy-boy husband, in between selling properties.

Chapter 8

Michael got up early on Thursday morning, pulled on a pair of shorts and a vest, and then pulled on some tracksuit pants over his shorts, put on a pair of gym shoes and headed off to do his surveying. Selwyn and Rob had filled him in on all the details and who to look for.

When he arrived at the gym, he found his way to the weights section and proceeded to pick up some fairly light weights, but all the time, keeping an eye out for the toy-boy as he had affectionately become known. It didn't take long for the young man to appear. When Michael saw him, he understood why it seemed laughable that such a hunky, young man should be married to this middle-aged woman, but Michael also understood the pulling power of money.

Michael watched as the young man started doing his repetitions and decided to go over, introduce himself and ask if the man wanted someone to help him in his exercises.

"Hi, there," said Michael as he neared the toy-boy. "Do you need a hand here with these weights?"

"Gee, thanks, my usual partner's not here this morning. I'm James Marriner."

"Hi, I'm Michael Bloomberg."

After the introductions, both men assisted each other during their exercises and moved together from one machine to another.

"I haven't seen you here before," said James, taking strain as he lay on the bench press and lifted his weights.

"No, this is my first time," answered Michael.

"Well for someone who's here for the first time, you've got yourself a pretty good body. Did you used to do gym?"

'No," chuckled Michael "It's just one of those bodies, you know."

"You're one of those lucky ones who is a natural and can attract anyone with his physique."

Michael laughed aloud.

"I wouldn't say that, but you look pretty good yourself. Have you been training for a long time?"

"For about four years, but I like to keep in trim. I always think that if you've got a good body, it always acts as a magnet."

"Do you find a lot of the women are attracted to you?"

"Sure, quite a few," replied James.

"I suppose you could score with any of these women here," said Michael, delving to find out any scandal related to James.

"It's funny you should say that, but between you and me, I'm not interested in any of them."

Michael wondered if this was a ploy to get him off the track, but somehow James sounded sincere about what he'd said.

"That surprises me because there're some hot girls here that I've seen. Have you got a girlfriend?" asked Michael.

James pretended not to hear him.

Then it was Michael's turn to lift weights and for James to help him.

"Are you married?" asked James, as Michael picked up the bar with the weights on.

Michael grunted as he did so.

"Was that a yes grunt or a no grunt?"

As Michael brought the bar back down, he heaved, "a no grunt! And you?"

Once more James chose to ignore the question.

"Tell me has this gym got a sauna here?" asked Michael, sitting up on the bench and changing the topic of conversation.

"Yes, would you like me to show you?"

"I feel like a sauna now that I've got rid of those heavy weights."

James laughed at Michael's comment.

"Those weights weren't heavy. You must try something heavier next time."

The two men wandered off in the direction of the change rooms and finally reached the sauna.

"Is this for both sexes or not?" asked Michael, pulling off his vest.

"No, this is the men's one. The women's is on the other side of the gym."

James bent over and removed his shorts and T-shirt that he'd been wearing.

"I don't know about you, but I hate wearing anything in a sauna," said James opening the door and entering.

Michael followed and the two men sat themselves down on the wooden benches. The heat surrounded them and soon they were beginning to sweat.

"Aren't you wet and sticky with your shorts on?" enquired James.

"It is quite sticky. I think I'll just whip them off."

Michael stood up and removed his shorts. Both men sat naked next to each other. Their conversation flowed on about gyms and body-building, but out of the corner of Michael's eyes, he could see that James was beginning to get an erection. The sight of James's cock growing erect became a turn-on for Michael, and instinctively he too found himself in a similar position. He tried to hide his embarrassment, but without luck. James noticed Michael's growing length and stretched a hand across and gently squeezed Michael's erection.

"That's quite hard and big," whispered James, as he gently stroked Michael's cock.

Michael wasn't sure what to do next. Here was the man he was supposed to be tracking, the man who was supposed to be having an affair with another woman, according to James's wife, and here was this buffed man coming onto Michael! Michael suddenly remembered that James had earlier said that he wasn't attracted to any of the women at the gym. Obviously not – James preferred men! Although Michael was enjoying the attention he was receiving, he felt he shouldn't be doing this, for two reasons: one - Selwyn wasn't there to join in and two, he was supposed to be spying on the suspect.

"Phew! It's hot in here," said Michael standing up, his erect cock bouncing as he moved away from James. "I think I need a little bit of fresh air," he continued as he opened the sauna door and exited.

Michael picked up his towel and wrapped it around his waist, just as James also emerged from the heat, engorged cock swaying in the air like an anaconda in search of prey.

"James. I must move it up, as I have to get back to work. It's been great meeting you and I hope I'll see you again."

"Where do you work, Michael? Maybe I can be in touch?"

Michael wasn't about to give out all his private details, but neither did he want to lie about himself.

"I work for a real estate company uptown, but maybe if we meet here again, you'll be willing to help me with my weights."

"Definitely. I'm usually here four days a week, Tuesday to Friday and at the usual time, which is early, before the others arrive."

After bidding their good-byes, Michael headed back to the apartment to get changed for work, but when he got home, he dialed Selwyn in Miami.

"Hi Selwyn, how are you?"

"Fine thanks. Are you back from the gym already?"

"Yes and do I have something for you and Rob!"

"What? Rob's right here."

"The guy's name is James and he's not into women. In fact he came onto me."

"What!" exclaimed Selwyn.

"It's OK. Nothing happened, but we were in the sauna and he started getting horny. The next thing he's coming onto me, so I left."

"And no women?" shouted Rob in the background.

"Tell Rob, he openly admitted he wasn't interested in them, so Mrs. Marriner doesn't have female competition, if that's any consolation."

"Thanks Mike," came the voice from Rob.

"How are you two getting on?"

"So far we haven't done much," replied Selwyn, "because we're trying to trace the boyfriend. We've managed to limit our area of search and we're hoping to track him down in a day or two, but in the meantime, you look after yourself and behave while I'm away."

"Yes boss," quipped Michael. "Love you!"

"Love you too," whispered Selwyn into the phone, obviously hoping that Rob wouldn't hear, and then the line went dead.

Chapter 9

In Miami, Rob had hired a car to get himself and Selwyn around during their investigations, and at the moment, they were on their way from their hotel on Collins Avenue to Lincoln Road, because they had a hunch that they might have some success near Lincoln Road Mall.

The area, on their arrival, was a teeming mass of people, wandering around, shopping, wanting to be seen and those looking at the passing crowds. Rob and Selwyn joined the throngs in search of their mystery man. Faces were everywhere and it was becoming impossible to distinguish one face from another. After a while Rob made a suggestion.

"Selwyn, we're wasting our time here, we're not going to have any joy here. Let's head back to the hotel and I'll make a couple of calls."

So Selwyn and Rob headed back in the direction of their hotel.

"Maybe we should go along Ocean Drive," suggested Selwyn.

"What did you have in mind?"

"Well isn't that where everyone who's anyone hangs out?"

"Oh, you mean the wanna-be and the wanna-be-seen people?"

"Yeh."

"Sure, we can do that. Let me have a look at that photo of our Mr. Browning once more, Selwyn."

Selwyn passed the photo of Byron to Rob.

"This guy looks like a kid."

"Well Gary said he was only twenty-two, but you know, what I can't understand is why Gary didn't want to go to the police about this matter."

"People are funny, Selwyn. It might have been because they were in a gay relationship and there are still many people who frown upon that, or it might have been that Gary's position in society might have been threatened if he'd gone to the police. You know what the media are like when they get hold of something. Look, if by tomorrow we don't have any leads, I'm going to call on a favor from a mate of mine who's in the police force here."

They drove along Ocean Drive, passing beautiful people of all shapes and sizes and Selwyn's eyes were everywhere, but not necessarily looking for Byron Browning. After driving up and down for quite some time, they decided to return to their hotel.

They had booked into a twin-bedded room so when they got back, Rob said that he was going to have a lie down, while Selwyn decided to take a swim. Selwyn slipped into his Speedo, picked up a towel and headed off to the hotel's swimming pool.

After splashing around alone in the cool water and then drying off in the glorious sunshine, Selwyn headed back to their room. He gently inserted the room key into the door and entered quietly so as not to waken Rob who might still be sleeping. Rob lay sprawled on his bed, flat on his back. He had pulled off his shirt and pants and lay in his tight white Calvin Klein briefs. Selwyn tiptoed around the room, but as he did so, he couldn't help but admire the muscularity of Rob. The man was a giant of a man and what lay cradled within the fine cotton of his briefs was the evidence of another giant. Selwyn could see the outline of Rob's lengthy cock and firm balls, tightly packed together. He felt an arousal in his Speedo and decided to avert his eyes so as not to embarrass himself any more than what he was already doing. Selwyn slipped his Speedo to his ankles and stepped out of it, wrapped his towel around his waist and then lay down on his bed. He lay for a moment admiring Rob's torso, the broad chest with a fine layer of hair covering it, and the tight abs that rose and fell gently as Rob breathed, then closed his eyes and dozed off to sleep.

Selwyn awoke to the sounds of the shower in use. The room was darkened and so he switched on a bedside light. He heard the shower stop and then heard Rob drying himself. The giant of a man emerged from the bathroom with his towel casually draped around his hips, but the protrusion in the front was very evident.

"Did you enjoy your swim?"

"The water was lovely and cool, you should have joined me."

"Maybe tomorrow, but I was just too tired, probably from the traveling."

"You looked like a baby when I came in after my swim. You looked so peaceful lying there," said Selwyn, lying casually on his bed.

Rob never reacted to the compliment.

"What do you feel like doing tonight?" asked Rob.

"I'm easy."

"Are you?" jested Rob, with a twinkle in his eyes.

Selwyn realized what he'd said. "I don't mean…"

"I know. I was only teasing you. How about having dinner and then going out for some drinks. How does that appeal to you?"

"I'm fine with that," answered Selwyn. "Let me just have a shower and get changed and then we can hit the bright lights."

Selwyn made his way into the bathroom and turned on the shower. The warm water cascaded over his lithe body as he soaped himself and ran his hands over his smooth body, caressing his chest, arms, ass and crotch. He slid his soapy hands along his slowly burgeoning cock feeling his foreskin slide back to reveal his glistening cock-head, then rinsed himself off without bringing himself to a climax. He switched off the shower, grabbed a dry towel and wandered into the bedroom with the remnants of an erection showing through the towel. Rob, by this time had pulled on a pair of jeans, a casual shirt and a pair of shoes and lay on his bed watching as Selwyn dried himself.

"You know you've got a very nice body, if you don't mind me saying," said Rob. "I don't know why you were going on so much about having to stake out in the gym."

"I told you, I just hate going to gym. To me it's a waste of time. Admittedly, I admire a good body on someone and I respect guys who are toned and in shape, but I haven't the urge to go through all that pain. But you've got a great body. I noticed it when I came in from the pool and you were asleep."

Rob laughed. "Oh you mean in all my glory."

Selwyn suddenly became embarrassed. Perhaps he'd overstepped the mark between them by commenting on his boss's physique.

"I think I'm too big," replied Rob.

Without thinking, Selwyn spat out, "I like big!"

"Oh!"

Selwyn stammered and stuttered as he tried to cover his faux pas.

"I was referring to my build, but you're right, I'm afraid I'm big in all departments, Selwyn."

"I know," he whispered, then added, "but it looks good."

Rob smiled and answered, "Thanks."

The conversation was creating an embarrassing situation for Selwyn as he was once again getting a hard-on so he hastily dressed in his jeans and a T-shirt and the two men set out into the night.

They decided to walk along the beachfront rather than drive as they had also planned to have a relaxing evening together. Italian was the meal of the evening and both men enjoyed their spaghetti and ravioli as well as each other's company. After dinner they wandered along the beachfront in search of a bar or two. They ventured into a couple where they sat chatting and downing their drinks - Selwyn his beers and Rob his whiskeys. The drinks and the conversation flowed freely. Both men were relaxed and enjoying themselves. Although they had quite a bit to drink both during dinner and in the bars they visited, they didn't have far to walk on their way back to the hotel. As they wandered back home, after they'd decided enough was enough, they needed to lean on each other for support.

Back at the hotel Rob collapsed onto his bed, laughing and talking non-stop.

"Come on Rob, it's time to get to bed. You'd better get undressed and climb into bed."

"I can't manage," slurred Rob. "You'll have to help me."

Selwyn staggered over to the bed and started undoing Rob's casual shirt. He managed to get the buttons undone, lifted the well-built Rob as best he could and get the shirt off.

"Come on pants now," laughed Selwyn as he unzipped Rob's jeans.

Selwyn pulled them down as far as Rob's knees then slipped off his shoes. Once the shoes were out of the way, Rob's jeans slid off easily.

"Right you're ready for bed," gurgled Selwyn.

"Now you," stammered Rob. "Off with those clothes."

Selwyn found taking off his clothes an easier task as he wasn't as drunk as Rob. He folded them and placed them on a chair in the room. All the while, Rob continued to giggle and chatter. Selwyn climbed under the duvet on his bed and turned to Rob.

"Can I switch the light off, boss?"

On hearing the word 'boss', Rob found this hilarious and roared with laughter. When he had settled down slightly, after the light was switched off, a soft voice came floating across the room to Selwyn.

"Selwyn, I can't get under the duvet. I need help."

Selwyn climbed from his bed and went over to Rob's bed. He tugged at the duvet on which Rob was lying, but it wouldn't budge because he was too heavy to be moved.

"I can't get it out from under you, Rob. I'll give you mine."

"Then you'll get cold."

"Oh that's OK. I'll be fine."

Selwyn took his duvet and covered Rob.

"Goodnight Rob."

"Goodnight Selwyn."

For once, silence reigned.

"Selwyn? Are you awake?"

"What's it now?" sighed Selwyn.

"Come and get under the duvet. You'll get cold in the night."

"I'll be fine, thanks Rob."

"I'm your boss remember. Now get here."

Although Selwyn had mixed feelings about spending the night in Rob's bed, he knew that he'd be happy to be snuggled up to Rob's strong body, so he crossed over to the other bed and slipped in under the duvet next to Rob. He could feel the large man's warmth exuding, and then he felt a muscular arm lie across his body. Selwyn froze where he was. Rob turned onto his side and as he did so, Selwyn felt the tell-tale hardness of Rob's erect cock nudging him in the side, and then he felt the huge hand clasp his crotch and squeeze. Selwyn couldn't control his feelings any more and soon both men were thrashing in the single bed, lips clamped securely together, erections rubbing up against each other's and their breathing becoming heavier and heavier.

Although Rob had indulged in whiskeys, he was still able to perform sexually. He lay on top of Selwyn - their mouths clamped tightly together, their tongues dueling to take control of the other's mouth. Rob broke free after some time and slowly began to slide down Selwyn's body until Rob's mouth found the long, hard cock of his new assistant. He sucked gently on Selwyn's pendulous balls, taking each one separately into his warm mouth, running his tongue over each and then sliding his tongue up along the underneath side of Selwyn's throbbing cock.

Rob's mouth then went in search of the magical entrance that he so desired. His mouth and tongue headed towards the puckering hole and on reaching it, Rob's tongue began a series of gentle insertions which were driving Selwyn crazy.

"Ooh! Please fuck me, Rob," cooed Selwyn, lifting his legs into the air to allow Rob easier access to his throbbing hole.

Rob needed no second invitation. He lubricated Selwyn with his tongue and then inserted a thick finger into the waiting entrance. Selwyn's asshole clamped shut on Rob's finger and the older man began a slow but gentle internal massage in search of Selwyn's prostate, which he soon found.

Selwyn's groans were becoming louder and so were his thrusts as Rob continued to massage the magical spot.

"Please!" moaned Selwyn, pushing his ass down onto Rob's finger. "I need you inside of me."

Rob removed his finger, leaned across to his bedside table, rifled for a condom, unwrapped it down his harden cock and aimed for the waiting entrance, As his thick cock-head pushed forward into the warmth of Selwyn's opening, his young friend sighed and opened up. Like a vacuum, Rob's thick cock was sucked into the warm chute and as it penetrated Selwyn, so he felt the young man's ass muscles clamp tight around his stem.

Throughout the night, Rob continued to plow into Selwyn's tight accommodating ass, pleasing both of them.

Early the following morning, both men woke simultaneously, arm in arm, face to face, crotch to crotch, and both still aroused.

"Selwyn, I'm sorry about last night, but I needed that."

"Thanks, Rob, but let's just say it was the booze."

"For you it might have been the booze, but for me I wanted that desperately."

"What do you mean?"

"I haven't been with a guy for a very long time and I was becoming frustrated."

"But you've got a son. You can't be gay!"

"Do you think because a guy has sex with a woman, that he cannot be gay? I was married to my son's mother, but soon after he was born, I realized that my marriage was a farce, so we got divorced amicably."

Selwyn had a strange feeling of excitement at finding out that his boss was gay and did so want to tell Michael, but if he did that, Michael was bound to ask how he had found out and that would mean divulging what had happened between them, and he didn't want to upset Michael.

"I assume that you and Michael are in a relationship," said Rob, still holding Selwyn.

Selwyn nodded.

"Are you going to tell him what happened between us?"

"I don't know."

The devil and the angel were once again sitting on Selwyn's shoulders. One half of him had given himself completely to Rob, uncompromisingly, but the other half was aware of the hurt he might create for Michael should his caring partner find out that he and Rob had made love together.

"I'm prepared not to say anything," reassured Rob, "but the decision rests with you."

Selwyn knew that this was not the first time that he'd been unfaithful to Michael and not told him, but he felt he couldn't control his urges.

"Rob, I can't tell Michael. I love him very dearly and I know he cares and loves me, but I have this problem – I like sex and I can't get enough. It's like a disease and there's no cure. You're not the first guy I've been with since Michael and I got together, but somehow we've got around this by both of us having sex with the same guy."

"Do you mean separately or together?"

"Together. I met a guy when I went swimming one day and then he came back to our apartment when Michael was at work. One thing led to another and ... well you know what happens."

"But the together?"

"We met him when we both went swimming and Michael liked him and invited him back home with us for drinks and the three of us ended up spending the night together."

"So, are you saying that as long as you two do it together with someone else, it's OK?"

"You could put it like that."

Rob thought for a moment, then released his hold on Selwyn.

"So for Michael to accept me sexually, we, the three of us, would have to have a scene together?"

Selwyn smiled and nodded. "Perhaps."

Rob continued to cuddle Selwyn as their cocks rubbed up against each other, while he switched on the TV in the hotel room. As they lay there listening to the news items that were being broadcast, Rob became more alert to what was being said.

"Selwyn, look at that picture," said Rob, pointing to the TV screen. "It's Byron Browning."

They both remained stunned as they watched and listened to the report.

An unknown assailant had shot Byron Browning in the early hours of the morning and the police were investigating.

Chapter 10

"Selwyn, I recognize that building. We passed it when we drove along Ocean Drive yesterday. That's where he's been staying. I'd better phone Gary Jackson and tell him," said Rob as they followed the TV report on the murder of Byron Browning.

"Do you think we should head to his place and see what the police are doing? Maybe we might find out some information," suggested Selwyn.

They both leapt from the bed and dressed, foregoing breakfast and headed along Ocean Drive. They drove slowly along Ocean Drive until they saw the yellow police barriers near the house in which Byron had been shot.

"Selwyn, we're going to have to play this cool. We don't necessarily want the police to block our enquiries, but we definitely need information."

When they arrived on the scene, they parked their vehicle and stepped out into the bright morning sunlight.

"Act nonchalant, Selwyn, just like the other onlookers."

They neared a policeman, standing guard near the entrance to the house.

"What happened here, officer?" enquired Rob.

"Keep back, sir," replied the officer, shooing the two men away.

There were others also standing nearby, so Selwyn approached one of the onlookers and asked what had happened.

"Apparently some wealthy young guy was shot in his house. I don't know if it was a break-in or a drive-by shooting."

"If it was a drive-by, where's the body?" asked Selwyn.

"Good point," muttered Rob to his assistant.

"He must still be in the house," said Selwyn, trying to get a little closer to listen to what the police might be discussing.

Rob pulled out his phone and dialed a number.

"Who are you calling?" asked Selwyn.

"Remember I said a friend owed me, well it's pay back time."

The phone rang and Rob waited for an answer.

"Hi Frankie, it's Rob here. How's it? Listen, do you know anything about this murder on Ocean Drive that took place last night or in the early hours of this morning? ... The dead guy's name was Byron Browning... Yes, that's the one... was he living with anyone that you know of? ... Uh huh! ... Let's just say I've got a client who's interested in Mr. Browning. ...look, I can't give you the details just yet, but do you think I could get access to the house to question the person who was there when he got shot? OK ... see what you can do. Thanks, I appreciate it. Cheers."

"What's the story?" asked Selwyn.

"There was someone with Mr. Browning when he was shot, another young man, but my contact didn't give me a name. Said there was apparently an intruder, but robbery wasn't the motive, by the looks of things."

"Rob, don't you think we aught to contact Gary Jackson and tell him what's happened?"

"Maybe you're right. Give him a call."

Rob handed his phone over to Selwyn who dialed Gary's number. The number just rang and rang. In fact it didn't even go into voice mail, but suddenly cut off.

"That's odd," said Selwyn, trying to redial.

The procedure was repeated.

"The phone just cuts off."

"Don't worry about him, Selwyn, we'll just continue with our investigation and then contact him when we have something more concrete."

They stayed watching the house to see if anything materialized, but nothing happened for some time.

"Don't you think we're wasting our time standing here?" suggested Selwyn. "What about your friend? Is he going to phone you back?"

"Who said it was a he?" replied Rob, with a wry smile.

"Then who is it?"

"It's my ex-wife."

As if on cue, Rob's phone rang.

"Hello, Rob Clayton speaking ...Oh Hi. ... Great, thanks ... when do you think we can get access? … Uh huh! … Uh huh! … We'll meet you on the corner of 11th Street and Meridian Avenue. We can take a stroll in Flamingo Park … ten minutes time will be fine. Cheers then."

Rob switched off his phone, took Selwyn by the arm and led him off to the car.

"Come young man, we've got a date with my ex-wife."

They drove to the appointed meeting place at Flamingo Park and waited for their contact's arrival. As they were sitting in their car discussing the murder, Selwyn suddenly gasped.

"Rob," he whispered. "Over there. Isn't that Gary Jackson? If it isn't it certainly looks a helluva lot like him."

Rob's eyes followed the direction in which Selwyn was pointing and confirmed that he too thought it looked very much like Gary Jackson.

"But what the hell do you think he's doing down here?" wondered Rob.

Just as they were watching the man walking out of the park area and heading in the direction of 12th Street, Rob's ex-wife arrived.

"Selwyn, follow him but don't let him know that you're following and then meet me on Ocean Drive at the Palace Foodbar. Now get going."

Selwyn slipped from the car and started following.

"Hi Frankie," said Rob, giving his ex-wife a hug and a kiss. "Thanks for doing this for me. I've just sent my assistant off after someone who looks like my client."

"Listen Rob, I can't get you into the house because forensics is still busy there, but I can give you details of the person who was in the house at the time of the shooting. It's a guy by the name of Brad Knowles. He's a small-time hustler. He's not there at the moment because they took him down to the station, but if you wait for him outside the station, I'm sure you'll be able to have a word with him."

"Thanks Frankie, I really appreciate your help."

"According to this guy Brad, he said there was an intruder. He and Byron were apparently sitting in the lounge having a joint when the intruder entered …"

"…from where?"

"Apparently from one of the rooms. He must have got through a window, but he didn't threaten Brad. He said the intruder just walked up to Byron pulled out a gun and fired two shots, then calmly walked out."

"And Brad, did he see any distinguishing features of the intruder?"

"He said it was too dark to see exact details."

"So were they sitting in the dark smoking their joint?"

"Must have been, if we're to believe his story. Now tell, me how are things with you?"

"Fine," replied Rob.

"And you love life? This young assistant you have, what's the scene with him?"

Rob laughed. "Do you mean, is he the latest guy in my life? No, he's purely my assistant, nothing more."

"If you say so," came the snide remark.

"Are you going to come with me to the Palace Foodbar, Frankie?"

"I think I better get back to the station, but keep in touch."

The two kissed each other and both set off in their different directions. Rob had always had a soft spot for Frankie and although they didn't see each other that often, they still remained good friends.

When Rob reached the Foodbar, which didn't take long to reach, Selwyn was already waiting.

"What have you got for me, Selwyn?"

Selwyn looked depressed and Rob knew what this meant.

"You lost him didn't you?"

"Sorry, boss. He ducked into an apartment block and I followed, but I couldn't see him anywhere, so I left because I had to meet you."

"Selwyn, I'm going to teach you something about investigating. It doesn't matter who you have to meet if you're following a suspect, you stick to the person, understand?"

"I really am sorry, but I'm sure we'll find him; he can't go far."

"That's what you think. Trust me, people who are on the run can disappear just like that," and he snapped his fingers. "However, tomorrow's another day and we'll find him. In the meantime, let's head back and have a rest; Frankie will keep us in touch."

Chapter 11

Meanwhile, back at the gym, Michael's body was aching from the previous day's exercising, but he had promised to help Rob while he was in Miami. Michael began with some light exercises to try to rid himself of his stiffness and aching muscles. To do this, he had decided to take in an aerobics class. The thump of music blared out across the aerobics room, while bodies bounced in time to the beat, Michael's included.

In the weights section, James had arrived for his daily workout and so had his usual training partner, a muscular man who obviously worked out with body building competitions in mind. The two stood chatting nonchalantly before starting to do their bench presses.

"Do you want to go first, Peter?" enquired James, pointing to the bench.

"Sure, if you don't want to," came the deep mature voiced reply.

Peter, the muscular gargantuan, stretched out his body on the bench. His pectoral muscles extended skywards, making his chest appear bigger, and each thick leg rested on either side of the bench. James stood at the head of the bench waiting to assist Peter in lifting his weights.

"Are you ready, Peter?"

Peter adjusted his lying position then gave James the cue to help lift the bar with its weights on. Peter's biceps tensed as he took strain and lifted the heavy weights. James watched in awe as Peter's chest swelled and his stomach flattened.

Michael's aerobic class ended and he ventured into the weights area, but seeing James with his partner made Michael duck back out of sight. He watched for a moment as muscles strained and arms bulged, and then made his way to the change room. He unlocked his locker and surreptitiously removed a small camera from his possession. He closed the locker once more, locked it and then made his way back to the direction of the weights section. By the time he reached there, James and his partner had swapped positions and James was now flat on his back picking up weights while his partner stood above James's head.

Michael watched as with each upward movement of the bar, James's hand grazed his partner's crotch. Michael could see the hefty package that filled the standing partner's Lycra shorts. As James's hand again grazed the bulge, Michael snapped a shot with his camera. Michael was well aware that taking photos of people in the gym was severely frowned upon, so he was determined not to get caught.

James and Peter continued their routine for some time until James felt he had done enough, both of lifting weights and grazing his partner's crotch.

"I'm going to hit the showers," said James, picking up his towel and leaving the weight area and heading towards the change rooms. Peter soon followed, but so did Michael.

When Michael entered the men's change room, he could hear the splashing of running water coming from a shower. He crept closer to the sound, and straining to peer into the shower cubicle, which had a three-quarter-length door, he could see two pairs of legs. He thought of taking a photo of the two pairs of legs but then thought how stupid that would be; because you wouldn't see the faces and then no one would know whose legs they were.

Undeterred, Michael sought a position above the shower area so that he could see into the cubicle and take a photo. He found a plastic chair, which he quietly took into the cubicle alongside the one that the legs were in. Gently he placed the chair on the concrete shower floor and gingerly climbed onto the chair. He strained to peer over the dividing cubicle wall and found that he was able to see the tops of the men's heads. It definitely was James and his partner, and he could see that both heads were in close proximity, like one might find when people were kissing. He positioned himself carefully on the armrests of the chair and found that he could now look right into the cubicle, so much so, that he could see them from head to foot.

Peter's arms circled James and as their lips met, so did their torsos. Their bodies writhed against each other under the flowing water and their groans were certainly not silent, even with the water splashing onto the concrete floor. Michael's camera was working overtime, but because of their intensity and perhaps the splashing of the water, neither James nor Peter heard the clicking of the camera.

Carefully, Michael dislodged himself from the armrests and quietly placed his feet back on the floor. The sounds coming from the cubicle were becoming more vociferous. Michael peered gingerly around the cubicle corner and saw both men in passionate embrace, their mouths devouring each other and their hands grasping any part of each other's body that they could find. Michael happily clicked his camera, but he was fully aware of how, by watching the two men, he'd become sexually aroused as well, and being naked in the shower area, if anyone came in he'd look very embarrassed.

The groans coming from the shower cubicle increased in volume and so did Michael's arousal as he watched James and his friend stroke each other's cock till they neared their climax. A loud gasp and a groan reverberated around the shower room as James and Peter climaxed together. After one last camera shot, Michael quickly moved back to where his locker was, wrapped a towel around himself and hid his camera. He went back into the main gym area and pretended to busy himself with some light exercises. He soon saw James and Peter emerge from the change room, both dressed and ready to leave. James never saw Michael, but as soon as the two men had left, Michael hastily dressed and hurried home.

Rob's mobile phone rang.

"Rob Clayton speaking. How may I help you?"

"Hi Rob, it's Michael."

"Oh Hi Mike. How are things your end?"

"Just great thanks. I've just got back from the gym ..."

"You're really becoming quite a gym addict aren't you?" joked Rob.

"Never! I was so stiff and sore this morning after yesterday's workout, but I managed to get some concrete evidence this morning."

"You mean about Mrs. Marriner's hunky toy-boy?"

"That's right. I took a camera to the gym and spotted him with his partner that you'd seen him with. Well one thing led to another and they were soon in the showers together, getting quite passionate. Any rate I managed to get some photos of the two of them in some serious embraces..."

"...You're joking! In the shower?"

"Yes, in the shower. I had to look over the cubicle wall to get the shots, but it was worth it. Now you've got what you want, but I don't know how dear old Mrs. Marriner's going to take this."

"Thanks Mike, you've really done me a great favor. I really appreciate it. I owe you one for this. Do you want to have a quick word with Selwyn, he's right here?"

"How have you two been getting on?" asked Michael, which caused Rob to wonder whether Michael had an inkling about what might be going on in Miami between Selwyn and himself.

"We're both fine, but we've had a setback because the guy we were here to find, Byron, got murdered last night..."

"...oh shit, that's bad. Now what are you going to do?"

"We're probably going to have to stay a little longer because we also spotted Gary Jackson, the guy who asked us to take on his case, roaming around Miami, but here's Selwyn. Cheers Mike."

"Hi there Michael, how are you?" enquired the soft-voiced Selwyn.

"Hi, babes. I'm fine but how are you?"

"Doing OK, but we've been pretty busy."

"Have you been behaving yourself?"

"Of course," replied Selwyn, adding a nervous giggle as he said it.

"Have you been to any bars or clubs since you arrived there?"

"Rob and I went for a couple of drinks, but that's all."

Selwyn thought it better than to say anything about his and Rob's night together, especially over the phone. If he were going to tell Michael, he'd do it face to face.

"Listen, I can't talk too long because I must get to work. I've got an appointment at 10:00, so take care of yourselves and don't get into any trouble."

"I'll try not to," said Selwyn, blowing kisses into the phone and then hanging up.

"You didn't say anything to Mike about us," said Rob, who'd been listening in to their conversation.

"I couldn't Rob. I didn't know how to tell him."

"Would you tell Mike?"

"I don't really know. Perhaps if you and he became closer friends, I might."

"And how do you think he might take it?"

"Rob, I really don't know, but I don't want to push my luck too far."

***

Michael showered and changed into his working clothes and drove off to the office. His appointment at 10:00 was to take a client to a vacant loft apartment that the client had shown an interest in buying. Michael was to meet the client outside the apartment block, so he set off in order to get parking. He arrived with plenty of time to spare, but was pleasantly surprised to see that his client had also arrived early. The only difference was that although he was expecting one person, the client and a woman had arrived.

"I hope you don't mind me getting here before time, Michael," said the client, "but I wanted to drive around to get an idea of what the area was like."

"And what's you view of the surrounding area, Chad?"

"I really like it. Oh by the way, Michael, I hope you didn't mind me bringing my Mum along for the ride?"

"Not at all. Pleased to meet you Mrs. Bradley."

They shook hands and all three made their way up the elevator to Unit 45. Michael inserted the key in the lock and opened the door to the spacious loft apartment. The windows were floor to ceiling with beautiful views over parkland. The beauty of this apartment was that there were no buildings looking into the units, so there was total privacy.

Michael gave Chad and his mother a tour of the apartment, pointing out its various features and then said that he would wait out on the patio while they had taken a private look around and had a chat about it.

Eventually Chad and his mother returned to where Michael was waiting for them. They thanked him and said that they would go away and think about it, however Michael was a little disappointed on hearing this because he was hoping that they might put in an offer, but that was part of being a real estate agent – things didn't always happen the way you thought they would.

"I'll give you a call, Michael."

"No problem, Chad. Nice to meet you Mrs. Bradley.," said Michael shaking hands with her.

"Likewise, Michael."

Chad then shook hands with Michael and left.

Michael had been on the road about fifteen minutes when his phone rang.

"Hello, Michael Bloomberg speaking."

"Hi Michael, it's Chad. Where are you?"

"Half-way back to the office, why?"

"I'm sorry to be a nuisance, but I was wondering if I could have another look at the apartment, if you didn't have another appointment to get to?"

Michael, sighed slightly, but inaudibly. Was he being messed about?

"Ok, Chad. I'll turn around and head back."

"Gee thanks. I really do appreciate that. I should be there in about five minutes."

Michael turned the car around and headed back in the direction of the apartment. When he arrived there, Chad was already standing outside, waiting; but there was no mother this time.

"Where's you Mum?"

"I dropped her off at home."

"That was quick."

"Sure, she actually stays very close to this area. I hope you don't mind me messing you about like this."

"Not at all."

They made their way back up to Unit 45, opened up and went in. Chad wandered over to one of the large windows and stared out over the parkland.

"Beautiful view," he remarked.

Michael joined him at the window. The two men stood staring out over the green trees and lawns.

"Could you see yourself staying in a place like this, Michael?"

"Absolutely. I think these units are some of the most stunning available, but don't you want to look around again?"

Chad headed off to the bathroom area and Michael followed. In the bathroom were a shower, toilet, washbasin and a Jacuzzi.

"This could be fun," said Chad, pointing to the Jacuzzi.

"Sure thing," echoed Michael.

Chad instinctively bent over and turned on the faucet. Water gushed into the tub.

"What are you doing?" asked Michael, wondering why the young man had done this.

"Don't you feel like having a Jacuzzi?"

Michael stammered as he'd never experienced anything like this before while showing clients around a property.

"Well I ...um... "

"I'm sure you'd like to because I know I'd like to try it out."

Very soon the Jacuzzi had filled with water. Chad never hesitated but ripped off his shirt, kicked off his shoes and socks, dropped his jeans to the floor and stepped out of his briefs. An athletically built man with a well-endowed appendage entered the water, sat down and activated the jets.

"Come on, climb in, Michael."

Michael hesitated again.

"Come on. It feels great. You'll like it."

"Let me at least lock the front door. I'd hate anyone to barge in on us."

Michael went back to lock the front door and then returned to the bathroom. The jets of the Jacuzzi were pumping water against Chad's back, as he lay almost in a trance..

"Hop in."

Michael undressed and slowly climbed into the warm water next to Chad.

"Now that wasn't too bad was it?"

"I suppose not, after all we have to try to please the client," remarked Michael, allowing the water to pummel his back as well.

They say chatting about interests and business, properties and sport. Every now and again, Michael felt the water push Chad's leg up against his and on some occasions, Chad left his leg pressed up against Michael's.

Chad had a pleasant enough face and was attractive physically. Michael had to admit to himself, inwardly, that Chad did have charm and charisma, and he also had to admit to himself that this young man sitting in the warm water alongside of him, was turning him on.

It was Michael's turn to have a hypothetical devil and an angel on his shoulders. One half of him was saying, *I haven't had sex for some time and it would be great to have it with Chad who's good looking and attractive,* but on the other hand, something within him said *it's wrong; wrong because of your job and wrong because you are in a relationship.* As he sat there contemplating the situation, he felt a hand grip his upper thigh. He froze. The hand didn't stay put for very long. It was soon sliding up his thigh until he felt the gentle grasp on his now erect cock. He closed his eyes, as though not wanting to watch. He could feel Chad caressing his balls as they floated in the water. He couldn't deny that the feeling was erotic, engaging and above all what he desired.

Michael stretched out a hand and reciprocated the touch on Chad, He felt the long, thick and hard cock of his client, waiting to be stroked, which he gladly obliged in doing. Chad threw back his head and moaned audibly. Michael moved to between Chad's legs, place both hands under Chad's ass and lifted him in the water until the engorged erection broke the surface. Michael eyed it for a moment and then like an eagle swooping on its prey, his mouth enclosed its girth and his throat opened to take in its full length. Chad's moaning became even louder the more that Michael pleasured him.

The water splashed; the jets pummeled their bodies, and their hands and mouths made music together until both men lay exhausted and spent in the warm water, luxuriating each other's company.

"Wow that was great, Michael. I bet you get a lot of guys being an estate agent?"

"What do you mean?"

"Well with empty properties you can bring whomever you like to these places and have a good time with them."

Michael laughed. "Chad you're the first."

"You're joking. I thought you guys did this all the time."

"Not at all."

"Then why did you do it with me?"

"I don't know. Perhaps it's that I just felt horny and you happened to be the right type of guy for me, but I don't know. Can I ask you something?"

"Sure."

"Please don't think me rude, but did you call me back to view the apartment or what?"

Chad smiled. "Both. I wanted to see the unit again, but I wanted to make contact with you. I would have said or done something if my Mum had not been around, and that's why I wanted to get back to you after I'd dropped her."

"I see."

"Is that all you can say?"

Michael felt a little embarrassed.

"I'm sorry, Chad, but I'm not used to doing this. I don't mean that I don't like having sex, but I have a partner and I don't usually have sex with every client I take to an empty apartment."

"I'm the one that should be apologizing to you. I can see that I've embarrassed you and for that I'm sorry, but for having sex with such a beautiful man such as yourself, I'm not sorry. Michael, the least I can do is tell you that I will definitely be putting in an offer for this unit, and I'm not saying that to appease you. I was going to make an offer; it's just that I wanted to see you again. Will you forgive me?"

"Chad there's nothing to forgive. I thoroughly enjoyed the time we had together and if I didn't have someone in my life already, I could see myself spending time with a guy like you, so please don't feel bad about it, it was good for both of us."

"So where's your partner?"

"At the moment, in Miami on business."

"So he left you all alone!"

"I think that's another reason why I was happy to please not only you but also myself. I miss him."

"And what's he do?"

"He's working for a P.I."

"Oh, Miami Vice!"

Michael chuckled at this comment.

"Not quite. Maybe his boss is that, but Selwyn's still learning the ropes."

Chad rose from the water, his elongated, subsiding cock dripped water from its tip.

"I've just realized we don't have any towels to dry ourselves."

"I suppose we could go and sit in front of the windows where the sun's streaming in and dry out there," replied Michael, also climbing from the Jacuzzi.

The two wet men made their way to the large lounge windows and sat on the floor. If anyone had a camera, it would have made a classic photo of two naked young men sitting drying off in front of a huge window, overlooking the tranquility of the park below.

Chapter 12

Rob's phone rang incessantly before being answered.

"Where the hell were you?"

"In the shower, Frankie, why?"

"If you're doing nothing tonight, I suggest you get yourself down to Lincoln Road to the club Score," suggested the female voice.

"Why what's that?"

"Just a busy, popular club enjoyed by the gays and lesbians here in Miami South beach area."

"Do you think I need to go and find someone to liven up my life?"

"If you feel like doing that, you don't need me to suggest it. No, I'm just suggesting that you might find it interesting."

"Why who's there?"

"I've had it on very good authority that Brad Knowles is there. You know the small-time hustler linked to the shooting."

"Oh yes, yes, I remember. Gee thanks Frankie. I really owe you big time. I'll take Selwyn down there with me and maybe we can get some info from the guy."

"Just be careful, that's all," said Frankie, ending the call.

Rob turned to Selwyn, with a broad grin on his face.

"Selwyn, we're going out tonight."

"Where to?"

"Frankie's just informed me that Brad Knowles the hustler is at a club so we're going to do a bit of investigating."

They headed off to the club, which by car wasn't very far from their hotel, and when they arrived they went in, the Giant of a man and the 'African-American Queen'.

Rob and Selwyn made their way to the bar and ordered a beer each. Once they had their beers, they sauntered around the club, listening to the Techno music blaring out of the speakers, looking for Brad. In one of the fairly dark corners, Rob spotted Brad.

"Over there Selwyn. The guy with the cut-off jeans and the tight T-shirt."

"Which one, Rob, there are so many that look like that."

"The one with the peroxide hair."

"Oh yes, I see. That's not too bad."

"Maybe not in this light, but I'm sure if we put the spotlight on him, you wouldn't look at him twice," replied Rob, advancing to the corner where Brad was sitting chatting to a guy who looked about in his mid-forties.

Selwyn followed and when they neared their quarry, Rob hesitated to listen to their conversation.

"Have you got somewhere to go?" asked Brad, rubbing his crotch in a seductive manner to entice the other man he was speaking to.

"We can't go back to my place because I've got someone there," replied the man. "What about you?"

"Listen, if you want a quickie, we can go back there into the toilet."

The man looked in the direction of the toilet.

"OK, it's better than nothing."

The two got up and headed away from Rob and Selwyn.

"Come on Selwyn, we need to go to the toilet."

"But…"

"…You need the toilet!"

Selwyn followed Rob as they followed the direction in which Brad went. When they entered the toilet, they saw that only one cubicle was occupied so Rob quietly knelt on the floor and gazed under the three-quarter length door. There were two pairs of legs, one in jeans and the other bare because of the cut-off jeans, which were not visible.

Rob indicated that Selwyn should enter the cubicle next door to where Brad was and to stand on the toilet seat and peer over the dividing wall, while Rob stood in front of the cubicle door, in case both men made a hasty retreat.

Selwyn peered over the dividing wall and saw Brad standing with his zipper down and his cock engulfed by the other man's mouth. Brad looked up and saw Selwyn.

"Fuck off!" shouted Brad.

There was a scrambling noise from the cubicle as the man stood up and the door opened, only to be confronted by the gigantic size of Rob. Both Brad and his customer stood gaping in the cubicle.

"What do you want?" shouted Brad, trying to sound authoritative and threatening.

"You!" boomed Rob. "You," said Rob, pointing to the customer, "beat it!"

The man scurried out of the toilet quicker than he had entered it. Rob moved closer to the cubicle and Brad tried to slam the door shut, but Rob prevented this from happening.

"What do you want?"

"Are you deaf? I told you, I want you."

"What for?"

Throughout this whole episode, Selwyn had remained perched on the adjacent cubicle toilet seat, watching the goings-on.

"I've got a couple of questions for you," said Rob, grabbing Brad by the scruff of his T-shirt and pulling him out of the cubicle.

"Are you the police?"

"No, not entirely."

"What do you mean, not entirely? You're either the cops or you're not."

"You're coming back with us for a little bit of questioning. We want to ask you some questions about Byron Browning. Remember him?"

Brad tried to pretend he didn't know.

"I don't know what shit you're talking," blurted Brad.

Rob continued. "The guy who got shot, but you didn't."

Brad struggled to free himself from Rob's clutches, but without success and Rob could see from Brad's behavior that his young victim was aware of what was happening.

"You're coming back to our hotel and you're coming quietly and without any fuss. We're going to walk out of here together, as though I'm your trick for the night, and Selwyn you're going to walk in front of us, out to the car. Clear?"

Brad nodded and followed Selwyn like a lamb as he and Rob walked out of the toilet and the club together. When they reached the car, Rob said, "Selwyn, you drive. Brad you and I are getting in the back where we might have some fun."

Brad timidly slid into the back of the car accompanied by Rob, while

Selwyn got behind the wheel and they headed back to their hotel.

Back at the hotel, all three went past reception and up to their room. Anyone watching would have thought that Rob and Selwyn had picked up someone for the night, and so they had, but for other reasons.

"Right sit on that bed," said Rob when they entered the bedroom. "Selwyn, lock the door."

Selwyn did as he was commanded and then he too sat and watched as Rob began to pump Brad with questions.

"I can only tell you the same as I told the cops. I didn't see anything because it was too dark," answered Brad, arrogantly.

"Were you a one-night stand with Byron?" asked Rob.

Brad never responded.

"Or were you having some sort of relationship with him?"

Again there was no response. This time Rob grabbed Brad by his shoulders and hoisted him from the bed. He threw him through the air so that he landed rather awkwardly in one of the two easy chairs in their hotel room. Brad landed with a thud and looked shocked by Rob's reaction.

"Right, now perhaps you'll answer the questions."

Selwyn sat fascinated by all this action and the more aggressive that Rob became, the more Selwyn thrived on his masculinity and manliness. The giant of a man towered over Brad, who cringed in the easy chair.

"Now what was your relationship with Byron?"

"We were having a scene together," whimpered Brad.

"Were you charging your usual rates or had you agreed upon a special long-term rate as it were?"

"I had moved in with him."

"Oh, so you weren't just hustling for sex, you were also enjoying the fruits of Byron's money, is that it?"

Brad never replied.

"Where did you meet Byron?"

"Along Ocean Drive. He was cruising there and he came by in a car, stopped and picked me up. He liked the sex and so did I, so we sort of hit it off together."

"You knew that he had money?"

"Sort of, from the way he dressed and the way he was throwing it about."

"Did you ever trouble to ask where his money came from; either inheritance or business or where?"

"I don't usually ask clients that."

"But you knew that he had money, so you decided to try and milk him, didn't you?"

"No, it was nothing like that. I told you we both enjoyed the sex we had and that was all."

"Have you ever heard the name Gary Jackson?" asked Selwyn, deciding to change the line of questioning.

Brad had a startled look on his face.

"You heard my friend here, do you know a Gary Jackson?" reiterated Rob.

Still no response from Brad.

Rob suspected that perhaps Brad knew something about Gary, so he leaned closer to Brad's face and was almost spitting in his face.

"Gary Jackson! Do you know that name?" hissed Rob.

Brad tried to back away, but couldn't go very far.

Rob grabbed hold of Brad's arm and twisted it behind his back, creating a painful position for the man, who yelped out in pain.

"Do you know him?" barked Rob.

Still nothing, so the arm was bent further back. At one stage Selwyn thought that Rob might break the guy's arm, it had been bent back so far.

"Yes," whimpered Brad, tears beginning to well up in his eyes.

"How do you know him?"

Another twist of the arm.

"I met him here," sobbed Brad.

"When and where?" boomed Rob.

"Last month," came a simpering reply.

"Last month!" exclaimed Rob. "Impossible."

"I'm telling you the truth. I met him here last month."

"Where and how?"

"He was staying at one of the beachfront hotels and he picked me up one night and took me back to his hotel…"

"..Yes, and then?"

"We spent the night together and then in the morning when I was leaving he asked me to come back the next night, which I did."

"And where was Byron?"

"I don't know."

"Wasn't he here with Gary?"

"Gary was in the hotel by himself."

"How often did you see Gary while he was staying here?"

Brad looked sheepish before answering.

"Every night."

"So you and Gary were having a relationship then?"

"Yes."

"But when did you meet Byron?"

"Only very recently."

"Did Byron ever mention Gary's name to you at all?"

"No."

"Did you know that they were lovers?"

Brad remained silent.

"I asked you whether you knew that they were lovers!" spat Rob, twisting Brad's arm again.

"Yes, yes. You're hurting me," whimpered Brad once more. "Gary told me."

"You know what I think happened? I think that you tried to milk the one and then the other of their money …"

"…no, no. It was nothing like that."

"Then how was it?"

Brad bit his tongue and wouldn't respond.

"OK, let's try this hypothesis. You were screwing Byron and Gary, literally and monetarily, and then you played the one off against the other and that's when Byron was killed, either by you or someone else, possibly Gary."

"I didn't kill him."

"Then who did? You claim you couldn't see because it was dark, but I'm telling you that you know very well who the killer was."

Brad sobbed uncontrollably, so much so that Rob slapped him across the face because he was becoming hysterical.

"Now control yourself and listen to me," hissed Rob once more. "If you don't help us, we can't help you. If you say you didn't kill Byron, who did? Did Gary pull the trigger?"

The sobbing continued, but now a little more subdued.

"I told Gary that Byron was milking him of his money…"

"…But you were the one who was milking both of them!"

"No. I had met Gary first and we got on very well, as I've already told you. Then Byron came on the scene and Gary became jealous. I tried to tell Gary that I preferred going with him, but Byron tried buying me, if you know what I mean. I phoned Gary and told him what was going on and he came down here…"

"…So it was him we saw," said Selwyn, interrupting Brad's train of thought.

"Where was I?" said Brad, trying to control his thoughts.

"You said Gary came down here," prompted Rob.

"Oh yes. Gary came here and told me to tell Byron we must have a night in together and that Gary would sort things out, as he said."

"So you and Byron were smoking together when Gary came in. Is that what happened?"

"Yes. While we were having a smoke, Gary came in and he and Byron started arguing…"

"…About what?"

"Gary accused Byron of ripping him off financially and Byron denied it, then Gary accused him of having an affair with me. That's when I got worried because I thought I was going to be dragged into their fight. Any rate they argued some more about stupid things and Byron punched Gary in the face. That's when I saw Gary snap. He started screaming at Bryon and threatening him. In the scuffle, I heard a gunshot so I fell to the floor and covered my face. By the time I heard no more shooting and had uncovered my face, Byron lay in a pool of blood on the floor and Gary was gone. And that's exactly how it happened."

Both Rob and Selwyn sat transfixed. By this time, Rob had released his grip on Brad's arm and the man was sitting slumped in the easy chair, mentally exhausted.

"What's going to happen now, Rob?" asked Selwyn, who was quite shocked by the whole story.

"Brad you need to tell the police the whole story, but you need to do it now so that they can put out a bulletin to apprehend Gary. I'm going to phone a friend of mine to come down and fetch you to go and make a formal statement, but I'll also explain what you told us here tonight."

Rob dialed Frankie and told her what had transpired. Within ten minutes a squad car had arrived at their hotel and Brad was safely escorted out of the hotel and taken down to the station. Although neither Rob nor Selwyn accompanied Brad, they told Frankie, as promised, what Brad had told them.

"Where do we go from here, Rob?"

"It's up to the police now, to get Gary, but I wonder why he asked us to take on his case?"

"Perhaps he was hoping that we might find Byron and get him back to Gary and away from Brad, but it doesn't really make sense."

"Do any relationships make sense, Selwyn?"

"I think so. Look at Michael and me."

Rob grinned broadly.

"Oh yes, look at you two. Apart from sleeping with me, without Michael knowing, who else have you slept with, without him knowing, hey? Then do you want to tell me the sense in a relationship!"

"You know, I would say that you sound like a bitter old man."

"Firstly, I'm not bitter and secondly, I'm not old," remonstrated Rob.

"Well, I actually think it's time that you did have a relationship with someone; it might do you the world of good."

"Ha, ha! Straight out of the mouth of the expert! Why would it do me the world of good?"

"It would be nice for you to go home to someone each night; to have someone to cuddle up to at night and someone to talk to when you have problems. Wouldn't you like that?"

"Hey, I'm happy the way I am, so don't even get ideas of trying to change me. Now get to bed because tomorrow we're heading back home. There's nothing more for us to do here. It's all up to the police now."

"Well, I'm going to have a shower and then hop into bed."

Selwyn had his shower and then hopped into his bed. Once Rob came out of the bathroom from having his shower, he hopped into his bed. Rob switched off the bedroom light and both men lay silently in their respective beds.

"Would you like to feel what a cuddle is like?" said a little voice from Selwyn's bed.

"Fuck off! You told me you were in a relationship!"

Chapter 13

Flying back home was exciting for Selwyn. He was looking forward to seeing Michael again, although they hadn't been apart for very long. He sat next to Rob on the plane discussing the whole Gary Jackson affair and wondering whether the police in Miami would catch him and if so, what would transpire.

"I'm sure that they'll get him," said Rob, watching the clouds below them fly past. "If they do, I'm sure he'll get a life sentence."

"But I find it so strange that he should have come to us to investigate his boyfriend."

"I think that was just a decoy in some way, perhaps to get us off his track somehow."

"But Rob, to me it still doesn't make sense. Why ask us to investigate his boyfriend in Miami, then go there and kill him knowing that we are going to be there when he does it."

"Maybe he didn't intend to kill him. Maybe he intended to have it out with the guy and then they could get back together."

Selwyn shook his head. "I don't think so. You see that brings us back to you not having a relationship. If you'd had a relationship you'd know about these things."

"What things?"

"Haven't you heard the saying, *hell hath no fury like a gay scorned?*"

"Sorry, but I thought it was a *woman scorned?*"

"Same thing! Obviously Gary knew that Byron was probably playing the field and decided he'd had enough, so he went down to Miami to confront Byron, who I'm sure was indeed milking the guy of his money; they had an argument and accidentally the gun went off and Byron died."

"So that's how it pans out in relationships?"

"Well not exactly, but sort of."

"In other words somebody in the relationship has to die when there's some cheating taking place?"

"No, not at all."

"So tell me, are you going to say anything to Mike about our night together, because if so, I need to know whether I'll have to investigate a shooting or something equally traumatic."

Selwyn glared at Rob, who had a slight grin on his face.

"Don't be silly. Of course we're not going to kill each other, or at least I hope not."

"Well you said that this sort of thing might happen in a relationship, so I just wondered!"

Selwyn remained quiet, contemplating whether he should say anything to Michael about the night of passion with Rob.

"So tell me, Selwyn, what are you going to say to Michael when you see him?"

"I'm going to fling my arms around his neck, hug him, kiss him and say how much I've missed him."

Rob, grinned at Selwyn when he'd finished explaining his arrival plan.

"You know what I mean," said Rob. "Or must I tell him that I made love to you?"

"Don't you dare say a word," exploded Selwyn, causing Rob to laugh at the pained expression on Selwyn's face.

"I'll think of something to say to Michael, but at the right time," replied Selwyn, who then went silent.

Selwyn remained quiet for most of the rest of the flight, until they landed, then he became talkative again as he excitedly looked out for Michael who was meeting them at the airport.

"There's Mike," said Rob on seeing him.

When they reached each other, Rob and Michael shook hands but Selwyn flung his arms around Michael's neck and kissed him lasciviously, as he had said he would do. Selwyn didn't seem to worry that people around them were gazing in disbelief at their passion.

In the car on their way back to the apartment, Michael said, "Rob, I've made breakfast for all of us so I'm taking you back to our place and then you can go home from there."

"Thanks. That sounds great. Then you can also fill me in on dear old Mrs. Marriner and her toy-boy."

As they drove back to the apartment, Michael wanted to know all the details of what happened in Miami. Both Rob and Selwyn regaled him with all the latest that they knew, but neither said anything about their night together.

"And what have you been up to?" enquired Selwyn of Michael.

"I've been killing myself at gym …"

At which both Rob and Selwyn roared with laughter.

"…My body is aching, but I've got all the evidence at home. I had the film developed, so you'll have documentary proof, Rob. But other than that, nothing exciting has been happening. Oh, and I sold a loft apartment while you've been away."

"Gee that's great," answered Selwyn.

"Thanks Mike for doing me the favor of tracking the toy-boy. I really appreciate it."

"Actually, if you want to know the truth, I really enjoyed it. It was exciting and fun. Ducking and diving from people to avoid detection was great fun and James never knew I was following him."

"And just how close did you follow?" laughed Selwyn.

"Well as I told you over the phone, I got great shots of him and Peter in the showers together having a great time."

"As long as you didn't join in with them," quipped Selwyn.

"I wouldn't have minded. It was really hot, and I don't mean climatically!"

Selwyn and Rob threw a glance to each other, but neither said a word.

Back at the apartment Michael had breakfast ready. They all sat down at the table to enjoy toast and jam, eggs Benedict, tea and pancakes. Rob explained his theories about the shooting to Michael, and Selwyn added his contribution about the time they spotted Gary and he gave chase, but lost him. Then it was Michael's turn to relate what happened in the gym and show them the photos. Yes, they were hot!

"You're a pretty good photographer," said Rob holding a couple of pictures and looking at them at different angles.

Selwyn looked at one of them and remarked, "Wow, this boy's big!"

Michael smiled at his partner, "If you say so."

"And you did nothing?" asked Selwyn.

"Just took photos."

"I wouldn't have been able to control myself if this was happening in front of me," commented Selwyn. "I probably would have dropped the camera and my shorts and joined in."

"I suppose it was tempting," said Michael, "and sure it did arouse me, but I knew I had a job to do for you guys."

Again Rob and Selwyn glanced at each other. They also had a job to do, but they had also found the time to share a night together, but neither said anything about it to Michael.

"What happens now, Rob?" enquired Selwyn. "Do we tell Mrs. Marriner about her husband or do we speak to him?"

"I haven't decided yet, but maybe I should speak to him first. Maybe by doing that, he might decide to let her in on his secret and end their relationship, or change his ways."

Rob continued to gaze at the erotic photos of the two men in the shower and both Selwyn and Michael noticed this interest. Rob looked at his watch and realized that it was too late to go to the gym to confront James as he'd have finished his training session, so he decided to leave it until the following day.

"Selwyn, I don't think we'll open up today, it's a bit late and I want to get home and relax a bit, so take the day off and I'll see you around 9:30 tomorrow. Michael thanks for the wonderful breakfast and also for your work that you did for me. I really am grateful."

With that, Rob excused himself and got a cab back to his place, leaving Selwyn and Michael to spend quality time together.

"Selwyn, did you see how intensely Rob looked at those photos? I wonder?"

"Don't wonder. Rob likes his men."

"How do you know?"

"In Miami, I met his ex-wife, so yes, he was married, but we got talking in the hotel and he told me that they had got divorced because he was more interested in guys."

"The way he looked at the photos, do you think he wants to have a scene with one of them?"

"Who knows!"

"But tell me, did you behave yourself with him around?"

Selwyn busied himself in the kitchen, washing their breakfast plates. Michael walked up behind Selwyn, wrapped his arms around his waist and pulled Selwyn closer to him.

"You didn't answer my question."

Selwyn put down the plate he was washing and turned around in Michael's arms. Looking Michael in the eyes, Selwyn replied: "We slept together one night because we were both drunk and didn't really know what we were doing."

Michael looked a little crest-fallen, but still remained hugging Selwyn.

"Selwyn, don't tell me that you didn't know what you were doing, drunk or not. If you get into bed with someone, you know exactly what you're doing. All I want to know is did you use protection?"

"Michael, it never got as far as that stage, so you've got nothing to worry about."

Michael stared hard at Selwyn.

"Knowing you, I somehow am not quite convinced with that explanation."

Selwyn hung his head and then answered.

"Yes we did use protection and afterwards Rob felt so guilty about it. He kept saying he needed it because he hadn't been with a guy for so long."

"And you, did you feel guilty?"

"Of course I did, but it was because I was missing you."

"Selwyn, I know about your problem. You have an overactive libido that needs to be satisfied. I understand that, but as I've said to you before, just take precautions if you have to go with someone other than me."

"Are you angry with me?" enquired a timid Selwyn, looking somewhat guilty.

How could Michael be angry when he knew that he'd been floating in a Jacuzzi with a client of his?

"I love you don't I? Therefore I'm a forgiving person," answered Michael.

Selwyn's lips pressed gently to Michael's and they stood there loving each other for a while.

"Would you like to take your soapy hands out of the sink for a while and come to the room?" whispered Michael into Selwyn's ear.

"I'd like that very much," was the whispered reply.

The two men, hand in hand, moved off to the bedroom.

Michael slowly and caringly undressed Selwyn and once he had removed both of their clothes, he gently lowered Selwyn onto their bed.

"I want to make love to you all day," whispered Michael as his lips touched Selwyn's.

As their bodies ground against each other, so their passion increased.

Selwyn gave himself over to Michael's passion and soon moans and heavy breathing were the only sounds emanating from the apartment as Michael sank slowly and steadily into Selwyn, thrusting deeply into the warmth of his lover.

In the middle of their passion, the phone rang.

"Leave it," gasped Selwyn. "They can always leave a message."

Michael continued to penetrate Selwyn, his perspiration dripping onto Selwyn's chest and stomach. The two men continued in the bedroom, ignoring the persistent ringing.

An hour later when both dragged themselves from the bedroom, Michael listened to the voice mail message.

"Hello Michael, it's your mother here, I was wondering if you and Selwyn would like to come round for drinks tonight at 7:30. Call me if you can't make it, otherwise if I don't hear from you that means that you're coming."

Michael and Selwyn listened to the message and both burst out laughing when they heard the last section.

"We're coming!" they both shouted simultaneously.

The two young men showered, and during the shower they continued to arouse each other with their passion, and once they had finished in the bathroom, they went back to their bedroom, collapsed back on the bed and began to make love all over again, until they eventually fell asleep in each other's arms.

***

The evening at Myra's was both pleasant and entertaining. Both young men told Myra of their investigating exploits, but obviously removed all sexual references so as not to embarrass Michael's mother.

"Doesn't anything exciting happen on these exploits?" asked Myra.

"But Mum, we've told you all the exciting bits," replied Michael, looking a little bewildered.

"What no sex, drugs and rock and roll type things? I thought P.Is had exciting lives falling in and out of beds, much like James Bond does."

"Mum, you're living in a fantasy world. It's all hard work, some of it dangerous. Selwyn, for example could have been killed in Miami."

"No, we can't have that, can we?"

Throughout this conversation both men were biting their tongues so as not to divulge what they considered to be the 'juicy' stuff.

"Don't you have any cases that have a little scandal in them? Nothing to brighten up a middle-aged mother's life?"

Selwyn and Michael looked at each other, smiled, then Michael proceeded to tell his mother all about James and Peter in the shower. If it shocked her, then so be it, after all she wanted scandal. Myra listen with glee, wanting more and more details, not so much of the case, but of the physical features of the two men.

"Mum!" exclaimed Michael. "You shouldn't be asking things like that?"

"For heaven's sake my boy, do you think I know nothing about sex. How do you think I gave birth to you? This was no immaculate conception. Your father and I always had passionate love-making together."

Michael began to blush at his mother's words.

"And what's more your father was well-blessed down in those regions. He always satisfied me."

"Mum! You don't have to go into the gruesome details."

All the while, Selwyn sat chuckling at Michael's embarrassment.

"You're just as well-blessed as your father, isn't he Selwyn?"

Suddenly Selwyn's smile disappeared.

"My boy's well hung isn't he?"

"Oh, very, Myra."

"And he satisfies you, doesn't he?"

"Absolutely!" replied Selwyn.

"Well there you see, it's the Bloomberg trait. Nothing to be embarrassed about. Now, how about refilling my glass?"

Michael leapt up and took his mother's glass off to the kitchen to refill. This was a moment of relief for him.

"Selwyn, is Michael looking after you?" asked Myra once Michael was out of hearing range.

"Oh yes, Myra, he spoils me."

"Good, because you seem a really nice young man and you seem to bring out the best in my boykie. I can see that he's happy and that always makes a mother happy. It doesn't worry me whether it's with a boy or a girl, so long as my child has happiness, then I'm happy. Now Selwyn, if there are any times that you need to talk, don't hesitate to come and see me. I know that son of mine, and sometimes he can be stubborn, just like his father."

"I've never encountered that Myra. I've always found Michael to be the epitome of kindness and caring. In fact, I think there are times when I'm more stubborn than you say he is."

"Well, just remember, any time, my boy."

Michael re-entered the lounge with his mother's drink.

"And what have you two been discussing about me?"

"I was just telling Selwyn how stubborn you can be sometimes."

"I'm not stubborn."

"As a little boy you were. Whenever he didn't get his way, he would stomp his feet, clench his little fists and grind his teeth."

"Mum, you make me sound like a monster."

"But you did do those things."

"Not any more, do I Selwyn?"

Selwyn laughed at the idea of Michael doing all the things his mother had said. "I'd love to see you doing those, but I've never seen it Myra."

"Oh well, maybe that's a good sign then. Perhaps he's changed for the better."

By 10:00 that evening, and having not eaten dinner, Michael and Selwyn made their drunken way back home. They undressed and fell into bed, arms around each other and immediately went to sleep, this time without having to resort to pleasure making.

Chapter 14

Birthdays! Always a happy time for some, but ultra depressing for others. People like Myra avoided having birthdays like it was some sort of plague, mainly because there would always be someone who wanted to know her age.

"I hate them," said Myra. "It's a time when you realize that you're little bit closer to dying."

"Don't talk rubbish Mum. But in any case it's not your birthday, but I'll call the birthday boy for you."

"Selwyn!" shouted Michael from the lounge. "Get out of bed; it's your mother-in-law on the phone wanting to wish you for your birthday."

A naked and sleepy Selwyn padded through to the lounge and took the phone from Michael.

"Hello, Myra," came a drowsy voice.

"Happy birthday my darling," chirped Myra over the phone. "And how old are we today?"

"Um ...twenty-five, I think."

"Mozeltov, my little goy and may you have many more wonderful years ahead of you."

"Thanks Myra."

"And what did that son of mine give you for your birthday?"

"I don't know because I've only just woken up and he hasn't given me anything yet."

"Not even a kiss?"

Selwyn merely laughed. "I'm sure he'll do that."

"Well I hope he does more than just that; you tell him I said so."

"Sure Myra."

"Are you having a party?"

"I don't know. If I am, then it's a surprise because again Michael hasn't said anything."

"Tell him he has to. Now listen my darling, I must be off. Busy day ahead – shopping you know, and hopefully I might see you later. Make sure that you have a wonderful day and that he treats you special. Bye, Selwyn."

"Bye Myra and thanks for the call."

Selwyn replaced the phone and flung his arms around Michael's neck.

"Mm! I'm so tired. Tell me, your mother called me her little goy, what's that mean?"

"It's Yiddish for a gentile or non-Jew."

"Oh, that's OK. I thought it might be some contagious disease or something. Oh and I have to tell you from her, that you have to give me more than just a kiss for my birthday; mother's instructions."

"What was she suggesting?"

"Use your imagination! You should know your mother. You and your long schwantz have to please me for my birthday, Myra's subtle suggestion, I would think."

Michael chuckled at Selwyn's expression.

"You'll have a special treat today, so don't worry about it, and tonight we're having a small party for you."

"Thanks, that's nice, but who are we?"

"Just me and a few friends. Now go and shower and get ready for work while I make breakfast for us."

Michael busied himself in the kitchen while Selwyn showered. While Selwyn was in the shower the phone rang again. Michael answered it and heard Chad's voice.

"Michael, sorry to phone you so early, but I wondered if you could make it to the loft apartment this morning?"

"Why Chad, what's the problem?"

"No problem, but I wanted to measure windows for curtains and as you have the key, I needed to get in somehow. Would it be possible?"

Michael wondered if there was an ulterior motive for Chad phoning, but what Chad had said was true; he did have the key and therefore had to unlock for Chad. Maybe Chad could call at the office and pick up the key, then

Michael wouldn't have to go with Chad, not that he had anything against the guy.

"Shouldn't be a problem, Chad. Would lunch time suit you?"

"That would be fine. Can I meet you there?"

"I'll be there at twelve," replied Michael, ending the conversation.

"Who was that?" asked Selwyn, entering the lounge with a towel wrapped around him.

"Just business."

"Have you got an appointment?"

"Yep. I have to take some keys to a client. You remember I told you I'd sold that loft apartment, well the new owner wants to get in to measure for curtains."

Selwyn never queried any more what Michael had told him, after all Michael had not been lying to his partner.

"And why haven't you dressed yet? You'll be late for work."

Selwyn immediately discarded the towel he was wearing.

"I thought maybe you'd like some of this!" he said flaunting his naked body in front of Michael.

"Not now, Josephine. We've got to get to work. Maybe later you might get lucky."

A despondent Selwyn sighed, picked up his towel and headed off to the bedroom to get dressed, while Michael watched the cute, tight ass waddle off before him.

At length, both men ate their breakfast, said their good-byes and headed off to work.

When Selwyn arrived at the office, Rob was already there.

"Happy birthday, partner," said Rob. "Am I allowed to give you a hug?"

"And a kiss if you like," replied Selwyn, taking the initiative as he hugged Rob.

He felt the gentle giant's strong arms wrap around him and then felt the gentle touch of Rob's lips on his. He couldn't resist the temptation and Selwyn slipped his tongue into Rob's waiting mouth. Rob was taken by surprise by this action, but it didn't stop him from reciprocating. The two men stood together for a short while, their mouths remained glued to each others, and then they parted.

"That was lovely," cooed Selwyn.

"You're right, it was," concurred Rob. "So what did you get this morning?"

Selwyn looked a little embarrassed by the question, because he hadn't received anything from Michael. Rob sensed that he's asked an awkward question.

"Didn't Michael give you anything?"

"Not yet. Perhaps I'm getting it later."

"I bloody well hope you get it later," said Rob nudging Selwyn. "But listen, Selwyn, I need to speak to James today about the photos and what he's been up to."

"Do you want me to come with you?"

"I don't think so. I'll tell you what, seeing that it's your birthday, you go off at lunch time and have the rest of the day free."

"Gee, thanks Rob. Maybe I'll meet Michael for lunch."

"That's a good idea."

As it was early, Rob made his way to the gym in the hopes of meeting up with James. When he arrived there, he didn't change into gym clothes as he wasn't intending to exercise. Instead he went to the juice bar and ordered a freshly squeezed orange juice. While he was sitting at the bar, he could see the weights section and would be able to see when James arrived. He didn't have to wait long, when he noticed James with his usual friend, Peter.

The exercises began and soon James was lifting weights, while Peter assisted him, then they swapped positions and James helped with the lifting. After about fifteen minutes of this, the two men headed off in the direction of the change rooms. Rob knew what was about to happen now, so he followed.

When Rob entered the change rooms, he heard water running in the shower area, so he followed the noise. He walked up to the cubicle where the door was ajar and the water was running and saw James and Peter together under the water.

"Excuse me, Mr. Marriner, I wonder if I could have a word with you?"

Both men glared out from the cubicle at Rob, but neither moved. Rob could see that both were sexually aroused, but he remained standing at the cubicle entrance.

"Who are you and what do you want? Can't you see I'm showering?"

"Mr. Marriner, I can see that you are both showering, but I think what I have to say to you is important, so could I please have a word with you?"

James heaved a sigh, grabbed a towel that was hanging on the shower wall and wrapped it around his waist.

"Now what?"

"I think it would be better if we spoke in private, if you don't mind."

James looked at his partner and shrugged his shoulders. Peter got the message and took his towel and exited the change room area.

"I don't know if you want to get dressed Mr. Marriner but what I have to say to you is of importance."

"I'm quite happy to stay the way I am because I haven't finished my exercising yet."

"Whatever you say, sir, but could we sit down?"

James led the way to a secluded spot in the change room and sat down on a long wooden bench. Rob followed suit. When they were seated next to each other, Rob spoke.

"I must say, Mr. Marriner, that you have a beautifully defined body, something you can be proud of."

"Thank you but I'm sure you didn't interrupt my shower to tell me that."

"You're right, but I just wanted to tell you that I admired your physique."

"Thanks."

"Mr Marriner ..."

"...please cut the mister business. My name is James, OK?"

"Sure, James, and mine is Rob."

"Fine."

"Right, James, I know that you are married and I also know how you like going with guys – there's nothing wrong with that, but I'm a P.I and your wife has hired me to check up on you because she thought you were having an affair with someone here at the gym. The only difference being that she thought it was with one of the women."

"My wife hired you to spy on me?"

"Yes James."

"And how long has this been going on?"

"Oh not very long. You see the minute I realized you preferred guys and not women, I decided to confront you and tell you what's been going on."

Rob pulled out his photos and showed them to James, who blushed profusely.

"Where did you get these?" asked an angry James.

"James do you deny that's you in the photo with your partner, Peter?"

He remained quiet, sill looking embarrassed.

"James, your wife has not seen these photos. In fact when I realized who you preferred, I chose to talk to you first before going to your wife."

"Thanks, but why would you do that?"

Rob smiled at James. "Because we have something in common, and it's not the same wife, if you know what I mean."

"So you're also …"

"…yes."

Immediately James seemed to relax.

"Now what happens? Are you going to show those to my wife?"

"Not if you make the effort to sort out this problem. I would say that you must speak to your wife and decide what you want to do with your life. Either you want her money, and I'm assuming that's why you married her, in which case you're going to have to make an arrangement with her, or you must get a divorce and be happy with the guy in your life, but the choice is yours."

James sat dumbfounded.

"Of course, if you choose to stay with her, I'll show her a photo, not necessarily a compromising one of you and Peter, to convince her that you're not having an affair with another woman. But I would suggest that you speak to her and iron out this whole thing."

"Rob I really appreciate your concern and I'm grateful for giving me the chance to set things right."

"James, for what it's worth, I used to be married until I realized that I preferred guys, so we got divorced. Admittedly there wasn't such an age difference between us as there is with you and Mrs. Marriner, but my ex-wife and I have remained the best of friends since then. She's got what she wants and although I'm not in a relationship, I'm still free to do what I want."

"You know Rob I think that maybe that might be the most reasonable thing to do. I'm living my life like a farce. I don't enjoy having sex with her, in fact it's become almost a chore, and I know I'd be much happier with guys like myself."

Rob handed the photos to James.

"I've kept this one of you and Peter kissing which I'll use to show your wife so that she can see that I did my job and the rest you do what you like with them."

"Thanks Rob. Do you think I could have your card, please?"

"Sure thing," said Rob, taking a card from his pocket and handing it to James.

"May I call you sometime after this is all over and maybe we could go out for a drink?"

"I'd like that, please. And I really am impressed with your physique."

"You look pretty big yourself," replied James. "Do you gym at all?"

Rob laughed. "Only when I have to follow you."

James laughed for the first time during their conversation, so Rob felt that the young man had realized his mistake and this made both of them relax more.

Rob stood up and extended a hand to James. "I hope things come right for you and any time you need help or want to talk, just give me a call."

"Thanks Rob."

Rob left the change rooms and on the way out he noticed Peter hovering near the entrance.

"I think James would appreciate your company and friendship at this moment," said Rob.

As he said it and passed by, he turned and saw Peter hurrying back to the change rooms. Rob got into his car and headed back to the office, driving with a light, good feeling. Being a P.I had its good moments, and this had been one of them.

***

Selwyn had phoned Michael to find out where he would be at lunch time and Michael had told him, he'd be on an appointment at the loft apartment. Selwyn knew where the loft apartment was situated, so he decided to surprise Michael by meeting him there and then they could go for lunch together.

Michael arrived at the loft apartment where Chad was patiently waiting.

"Thanks so much for letting me get in and measure the windows, Michael."

They made their way up to the loft and Michael unlocked. The two went in and Chad immediately got busy, with the help from Michael of measuring the windows.

When they had completed their task, they were standing in the kitchen chatting when Chad made a move towards Michael. He pulled Michael towards him, put his hand behind Michael's head and planted a kiss on his lips. Michael was taken by surprise and tried to fight Chad off, but the grip of Chad's was strong. Michael could feel the man's tongue fighting to enter his mouth and he could feel how Chad was grinding his pelvis against Michael's. Slowly he felt something hard pressing up against him and Michael knew what it was. Chad was all over Michael. His hands were wandering and caressing over Michael's body, and his mouth was on Michael's neck and then ears and then mouth.

"Anyone here!" shouted a voice.

Immediately Michael broke free from Chad's clutches. He recognized the voice.

"In here," shouted Michael.

Selwyn walked into the kitchen while Chad pretended to be drinking from a tap at the basin.

"This is a nice surprise," said Michael, relieved to see his partner.

"I thought I'd surprise you and go for lunch from here," said Selwyn.

"Um, Selwyn let me introduce you to my client, Chad. Chad this is Selwyn."

The two glanced at each other, but Selwyn glanced longer than Chad.

"Well, I'd better be going Michael. Thanks for unlocking for me and helping with the measuring. I'll give you a call some time."

"Sure," replied Michael, as Chad left the loft apartment.

"That's not bad looking," said Selwyn, grinning at Michael.

"Oh yes, very nice, but a little bit overpowering sometimes."

"Why, what do you mean?"

"Thanks for coming in time. I was almost being raped."

"What! By him? My God, you're lucky. Nobody that good-looking ever rapes me."

"I'm not joking. He was all over me."

"So you should have just gone with the flow, Michael."

"Selwyn, you know I'm not like you who wants to bed every second man who passes by."

"You're wrong, it's not every second guy; it's every guy who's good-looking. But enough of this, it's my birthday and we're going out for lunch so let's hit the road."

They found a small, cozy restaurant where the two of them sat quietly enjoying their midday meal and each other's company, and then after lunch, headed home for a rest.

"Am I getting a birthday party or not?" asked Selwyn.

"Do you think you deserve one," enquired Michael, "after what you put me through?"

"Truthfully? Yes!"

Michael smiled and took both Selwyn's hands in his.

"Well you're having a few guests tonight."

"Who's coming?"

"You, me, Rob and Greg. Just the four of us. I did think of inviting my mother, but then I thought she might make a pass at Rob or Greg and that could be embarrassing. So let's have a rest and then tonight we'll be fresh for your party."

Chapter 15

Michael had decided to treat Selwyn to a low-key party with only their close friends, albeit new friends. He could have organized something at the club where Selwyn still performed, but he wanted something intimate. Michael had made a few snacks and had also bought some, along with some beers and whiskey.

"Why the whiskey?" asked Selwyn.

"You never know if my mother pitches up and Rob enjoys the odd whiskey."

Both men had showered and dressed. Selwyn looked extremely smart in a pair of black leather jeans into which was tucked a white Armani shirt, while Michael had on his ordinary jeans and a T-shirt with *I'm Available* written across the front.

"Are you hoping to be picked up by someone tonight?" asked Selwyn when he spotted what was written on Michael's shirt.

"I might ask you the same question, wearing those tight, revealing leather jeans, which by the way do wonders for you."

Selwyn was extremely flattered by the compliment.

"I'm only trying to attract you," he said, running his hands seductively over his tight ass.

"Did you invite your Mum, Michael?"

"No, but do you want me to? It wouldn't take her ten minutes to get dressed and speed over here."

"I think she was hoping for a party and to be invited," replied

Selwyn.

"Fine, then let me give her a call."

Michael immediately dialed his mother's number.

"Hi Mum. Are you busy doing anything tonight?"

"No, why my boy?"

"Selwyn and I wondered if you'd like to pop round for a bit of a party."

"Why, haven't you got any guests pitching up, so now you want your mother to make up the numbers?"

"Not at all, Mum. We'd both like you to join us. We've only invited two other friends to come along, so with you there'll be five of us."

"A bit of an odd number isn't it?"

"Does it matter, or were you hoping to catch someone tonight for yourself?"

"You mustn't underestimate your mother. She hasn't lost her touch you know."

Michael laughed at this comment and told her to stop wasting time and to get round to their apartment.

"Be here by 7:30 Mum. I must run and get things ready. See you soon. Bye."

Michael hung up and went to help Selwyn with the preparations.

"I told her to be here by 7:30, but knowing my mother, she'll be here by 7:00. You know Selwyn, I have to honest with you that you really look good in those leathers, but then you look good in anything."

"Thanks. I really appreciate that. If I look so good in anything, do you think I should go and get changed into some drag? That'll confuse your Mum. You could tell her that you've dumped me and decided to go straight and you're now having an affair with Selwyn's sister. How do you think she'd take that?"

"I really don't know. I think she's accepted the fact that I'm gay and in a relationship with you, so to confuse her poor little mind might damage her for life. Mind you, it would be good for a laugh."

"Shall I do it, then?"

"No. I prefer the leather look. That look could win you surprises in bed tonight!"

Fifteen minutes after the phone call to Michael's Mum, there was a knock at their front door. Selwyn opened it and there stood a ravishing Mrs. Bloomberg.

"Wow! Have you got a date tonight Myra. You're looking absolutely fabulous."

"You never know who I might bump into tonight and I want to look good for them. By the way, you look stunning. Was this your idea to wear leathers or Michael's?"

"Mine. I wanted to surprise Michael."

"And what's his reaction been like?"

"I'll tell you tomorrow, but he did promise surprises in bed tonight."

"Oh that terrible son of mine," chuckled Myra. "Selwyn, here's a little something for you," and she handed him an envelope.

"Thanks Myra but you didn't have to worry about a gift."

"Oh, but I'm not worrying about it. You use to get something you need."

"Hi Mum, thanks for coming round," said Michael coming from the kitchen and giving his Mum a kiss on the cheek.

"I wouldn't miss this for the world," replied Myra. "Now tell me, who's coming tonight and are they gorgeous?"

"Mum it's just a couple of our friends, that's all."

"Yes, but are they candy for the eyes?"

"Ask your son-in-law."

"Well Selwyn, are they?"

"I think so," answered Selwyn, "especially my boss."

"Oh is your boss coming? Does he know about you two boys?"

Selwyn and Michael threw each other a glance.

"Yes Mum and the other person coming is just a fairly new friend of ours."

"And what does he do?"

Once more the two boys glanced at each other. They actually didn't know what he did.

"I don't know, Mum."

"You don't know, but you say you're friends of his? That sounds odd to me."

"Well, we've never bothered to ask. Oh, and Mum, please keep the interrogations to a minimum."

"What do you mean? I never interrogate anyone."

Both Selwyn and Michael laughed uproariously while Myra looked at them with surprise.

"I really don't know why you're laughing, because it's true. When have I ever interrogated either of you?"

"Mum, we won't go down that route. All I'm asking is that you keep the questions to a minimum and keep your comments clean."

Myra looked somewhat indignant at Michael's request, but assured them that she wouldn't embarrass them.

Rob was the first guest to arrive, bringing with him a bottle of Cabernet wine, which he handed to Selwyn and without Myra seeing, gave him a kiss on the cheek.

"Happy birthday, again, Selwyn."

"Thanks Rob. Michael, won't you put the wine in the kitchen and we can open it later?"

"Myra can I introduce you to my boss. This is Rob Clayton. Rob, this is Michael's Mum, Mrs. Bloomberg."

"Myra!" interrupted Michael's Mum, as she seductively extended her hand as though for Rob to kiss.

Rob dutifully obliged. Myra blushed and whispered, "Charmed."

"Take a seat, Rob, and what would you like to drink?" asked Selwyn.

"I'd love a cold beer, if you have, please."

"One beer coming up," said Michael, going off to the kitchen.

"And what about me?" shouted Myra as Michael left the lounge.

"Your whiskey's on its way, Mum," came the reply from the kitchen.

Rob sat himself down on the couch and no sooner had he done so than Myra joined him there.

Michael returned with a tray of drinks; beers for the boys and whiskey for Myra.

"Rob, please just watch my mother. If her hands start wandering, slap them and if she makes a proposition to you, well, then you decide what to do about her," said Michael handing Rob and Myra their drinks.

"You see how my son speaks to his mother?"

"But I'm sure that he loves you, Myra."

"Of course I do, don't I Mum?"

"I suppose he does."

"Who else is coming?" enquired Rob.

"Just another friend of ours," replied Selwyn.

"Now tell me Rob," started Myra, edging a little closer along the couch towards Rob. "I believe you're a P.I," she stated in a seductively deep voice. "You must see some strange things in your line of work."

"You could say that," responded Rob.

"Like what?" asked Myra, beaming angelically at Rob.

"Rob, watch it. My mother loves a bit of scandal."

Rob chuckled and smiled back at Myra.

"I don't think you'd be interested in what I see sometimes."

At this, both Selwyn and Michael guffawed.

"Rob, you don't know my mother, so you'd better spill some beans just to make her happy, otherwise she's going to nag you all night."

Rob took a sip of his beer as if to procrastinate.

"My boy, you're playing for time, I know it," said Myra, as a mother might say to her naughty child.

Rob laughed. "You're right there. Well I often have to spy on husbands and boyfriends, cheating on their wives or girlfriends."

"And...?" replied Myra, waving her hand as though to tell Rob to carry on.

"And ... sometimes I have to spy on the wives as well."

"Ooh, you have to watch some of those women. You should hear the stories that I hear when I go to the hairdressers! What some of those women get up to, I'm not surprised you're in business."

All four of them were now sitting enjoying their drinks and Myra was like a dowager duchess holding court. She sat erect on the couch, regaling the men in the room of hair-raising hairdressing stories.

"Michael you know Mrs. Jankowitz who used to live near us, well she's been having an affair with her pool cleaner. Apparently, when her husband goes off to work, the pool cleaner starts his work, and I don't mean cleaning the pool; that only comes later."

"Mum! Do you really think you aught to be talking like that about people?"

"Well, it's true. She is having an affair. Look, I don't blame her because I've seen him and he looks very nice. It's just a pity I don't have a pool," she added as an afterthought.

All three men giggled at Myra's comment, but it didn't stop her. She was on a roll.

"And you remember the woman who lived next door to us when you were about seventeen or eighteen? You know the one whose son was in your class at school? Well she caught her husband with the maid."

"Mum!"

"It's true. Don't you remember the incident?"

"Mum it wasn't the husband with the maid, it was the son."

"Oh! Oh well, that's not so bad then. No, I think being a P.I must be so exciting. Aren't you finding it exciting, Selwyn?"

"Very, especially when you have a murder on your hands."

"You've had a murder! That's most awful," continued Myra, "but tell me about it."

She was like a child, totally enwrapped by the stories that either Selwyn or Rob was willing to tell her. So long as it sounded scandalous, she was happy.

"Michael, another drink please. I just love listening to these stories."

Michael dutifully went and got his mother another whiskey and brought it back to her. Although Michael also found some of the stories interesting, he felt it was Selwyn's night so he should be the focus of attention, not his mother, but there was no stopping her.

While Myra was digging for more information from Selwyn and Rob, there was a knock at the front door.

"That must be our other guest," said Michael getting up and going to the front door.

He opened the door and Greg stood there, shampooed, shaved and looking smart. Although he was casually dressed, he had an air of elegance and seductiveness about him.

"Hi Greg, you look really great tonight."

"Thanks, Michael. Do I get a kiss?"

"I'm sorry," apologized Michael, giving Greg a kiss and a hug.

"So where's the birthday boy?"

"Oh he's busy entertaining my mother and a friend in the lounge. Come in and join them."

Michael led Greg through to the lounge where the others were laughing and joking about something that Rob had said.

"Oh, hello," said Myra, looking up and seeing Greg. "You look very handsome."

"You must excuse my mother, Greg, but she makes passes at all my men friends. Mum, Rob, this is Greg. Greg this is my Mum, Myra and this is our friend, Rob."

"Pleased to meet you Myra," replied Greg, shaking hands with Myra. "Hello Rob. Long time no see."

"Do you two know each other?" enquired Selwyn.

"We go back a long time, but we won't go there," said Greg a little tensely.

Rob merely glanced his way; a glance that didn't go unnoticed by Selwyn and Michael.

"Come and sit on the couch next to me, Greg. I want the two most handsome men on either side of me," commanded Myra.

Greg sat down next to Myra who instinctively placed a hand gently on

Greg's thigh.

"Now tell me Greg, where do you know Rob from? I hope you weren't a missing person and he had to find you or something like that."

Both Greg and Rob became uncomfortable and Michael noticed this.

"Mum, how many times have I told you not to interrogate my friends?"

"Darling, I'm not interrogating, I'm merely interested. There is a difference isn't there Rob?"

Rob was suddenly woken from his trance-like state.

"Oh, sorry … yes."

"To answer your question Myra, I suppose you could say that I was a missing person and Rob found me," replied Greg.

"Oh how exciting," responded Myra. "How come you were missing?"

"Well I wasn't physically missing, as you might say; I was just missing something in my life."

Michael and Selwyn glanced towards each other. Was this what they were thinking? That perhaps Greg and Rob had a relationship together at some stage?

"Oh dear, I don't understand," retorted Myra.

"Rob and I used to be in a relationship together."

There was an audible gasp from Myra and a shocked but understanding look from both Selwyn and Michael.

"So what happened?" continued Myra.

"We just decided that it wasn't for us," interrupted Rob, "so we went our different ways."

"What a pity, because you both seem such nice young men," said Myra.

"Rob you told me once that you had been in a relationship. Was that relationship with Greg?" asked Selwyn.

Rob smiled as though he had suddenly been transported back to the time that he and Greg were together.

"Yes."

"I think you aught to get back together," said Myra, taking charge again.

"Mum you can't just manipulate people's lives like some Yiddisher match-maker," countered Michael, trying to take away some of the embarrassment that Greg and Rob were going through. "If Greg and Rob wanted to get back together, they can decide after discussing their feelings with each other. It's not for us to say what they must do. You're beginning to sound just like George W. Bush, confused."

"What do you mean, son?"

"He said that America was a free society, but it didn't mean that they had to redefine traditional marriage."

"I don't remember him saying that."

"Way back in 2004 in Pennsylvania, I think," replied Michael. "So leave it to Greg and Rob, OK?"

"Whatever you say, Michael."

"Greg we haven't even got you a drink yet. What would you like?" enquired Selwyn.

"A beer if you have. And what's more, I haven't even wished the birthday boy. Come here."

Greg stood up and hugged and kissed Selwyn, wishing him for his birthday, and then sat down again next to Myra, while Selwyn went off to the kitchen to get Greg's beer.

"Where did you two meet?" asked Myra, not giving up on her venture.

"Mum! Let it go. This is not the Spanish Inquisition, you know."

"It's OK with me," rejoined Rob, "if it's OK with Greg."

"I don't mind talking about it. It's something in the past."

"So, where did you meet?"

"In a club," responded Rob. "I had gone out after my divorce and I was standing at the bar when I got chatting to Greg, who happened to be standing next to me. He looked lost because, at the time I didn't know, but he'd also just gone through a divorce…"

"… Oh how romantic; two divorcees," chirped Myra.

"Well one thing led to another and we were soon dating each other, but we never reached the stage like Selwyn and Michael, to move in together."

"Why ever not. You seem so suited to each other," said Myra with a perplexed look on her face.

"I don't know," continued Rob. "Maybe it was that we didn't think it right at the time. Also in those days, we had to keep a little circumspect about our relationships; I don't know."

"And you Greg?" enquired Selwyn, who had returned with Greg's beer and a few snacks on a tray.

"I wasn't one hundred percent sure that I was doing the right thing. I had this confused mind. Was I gay or wasn't I? I knew that I liked going with guys, but did it warrant having a full-time relationship; that I didn't know, so I suppose I was happy to let it go and stay single."

"How tragic," whined Myra. "It sounds almost like something out of a Shakespeare play where the lover must die because of some transgression."

"It's choices, Mum. We all have them in life and if that's what Greg and Rob wanted, who are we to condemn them?"

"When last did you two see each other?" asked Selwyn, now as fascinated by this revelation as Myra was.

"I don't know," said Greg. "Perhaps as long as ten years ago."

"I think it's more," suggested Rob, "but I must confess, I have seen you a couple of times around town, Greg."

"And you didn't say anything?"

"I thought you might be angry or something, so I let it be."

"I'm sorry you didn't say something to me. I really have missed you, even if only for the friendship."

"There you are," cried an elated Myra. "That's the start of something good coming out of tonight."

"Mum! Nothing good comes from things that are forced," said a despairing Michael. "Guys, you must excuse my Mum because she's like a Terrier or a Bulldog; once she latches on to something, she never lets go!"

"I just think it's sad that these two good-looking men have wasted so many years apart when they were both suffering internally," responded Myra.

"Enough Mum. Come and help me get the warm snacks in the kitchen and leave these two poor men alone for a while."

"Oh, do I have to? I'm supposed to be a guest."

"Come on," repeated Michael.

He stood up and took his mother's hand and led her off to the kitchen where, hopefully, she'd be out of harms way. This move left Greg and Rob sitting together on the couch, with Selwyn watching them. For a moment there was an uncomfortable silence, and then Rob's phone broke the tension by ringing.

"Excuse me," he said, standing up and moving away from Greg and Selwyn. "Hello, Rob Clayton speaking ... of hi Frankie. What's the problem? ... Huh Huh ... Oh good work ... I'll tell Selwyn. Thanks again and take care. Bye." He terminated his call and sat back on the couch.

"Frankie says happy birthday, Selwyn."

"Thanks Rob, but how did she know it was my birthday?"

"I phoned her earlier today and told her I would be at your place because it was your birthday; and they've caught the guy."

"Great job; that was quick," replied Selwyn. He then saw the puzzled look on Greg's face. "Just a case Rob and I were on down in Miami."

"Oh, I see. I think I'll have to go down there tomorrow or the day after," murmured Greg.

"Business or pleasure?" asked Rob, loosening up a bit to Greg.

"Business I'm afraid, by the sounds of it. Apparently my son's in some trouble. You know what these young kids are like!"

"Nothing too serious I hope," continued Rob, with a tone of sincerity in his voice.

"Something about him being arrested. As I was coming up in the elevator here, I got a call from him."

"I'm sorry to hear that, Greg," replied Rob. "I've got a contact in the force down there, who might be able to help if you need it; it's my ex-wife."

"Thanks Rob, I appreciate the offer, but I won't be able to do anything until I get down there and find out exactly what's been going on."

"Well give me his name and I can call my ex-wife and should you need help down there, I'm sure that she'll help you."

"OK, thanks Rob, his name is Gary Jackson."

It was as though a bullet had been fired and hit Rob between the eyes. He stared at Greg, then turned to Selwyn.

"Sorry, but what did you say his name was?" requested Rob.

"Gary Jackson."

"But Greg, your surname is not Jackson, or at least it wasn't when we first met."

"No, Rob, after my divorce, Gary chose to take his mother's maiden name, which was Jackson."

Both Selwyn and Rob were stunned and neither knew exactly what to say to Greg. They could tell him the truth, or they could keep quiet and let Greg go to Miami. Just then Michael and Myra re-entered the lounge carrying hot snacks. There was a deathly silence that greeted them.

"Please, your excitement and enthusiasm is overwhelming me," quipped Michael, "in fact I am being deafened by all the cheering for hot food."

Still the atmosphere remained icy, so much so that it could have been cut with a knife.

"Why the silence?" asked Myra. "Did somebody fart?"

That comment broke the ice and everyone either smiled or laughed. That was the moment that Rob decided not to say anything to Greg, at least not among the present company. The food was laid out on the coffee table and everyone tucked in, forgetting what had previously been the topic of conversation.

"This is delicious. Did you make this, Michael?" asked Greg, taking a bite into a savory tart.

"I suppose I could lie and take the credit, but no, I didn't make it, and might I add, before you give any one else compliments, neither did Selwyn or my Mum."

"Well, wherever it came from it's really tasty, in fact it tastes like more."

"You tuck in, Greg," encouraged Myra. "Come on Rob, have some and try it."

Rob obliged by trying some of the tart and he too paid the necessary compliments. Then he asked where the bathroom was.

"I hope it's not Michael and Selwyn's food that's making you want the bathroom," giggled Myra.

"No, Myra, it's actually the beer. Selwyn could you show me where the bathroom is?"

Selwyn and Rob went off in the direction of the bathroom, and it was here that Rob suggested to Selwyn that they say nothing to Greg about Gary, but that he might tell Greg later that night, perhaps when they were leaving. Selwyn agreed.

"Tell me, Greg, what do you actually do, work wise I mean?" interrogated Myra again.

"I have my own business."

"Oh, like Rob here. Having your own business always allows you so much more independence, doesn't it," continued Myra

"Not always," retorted Michael. "You might have the joy of not having to work for someone else, but you have very little time to yourself."

"I don't know, Michael," related Greg. "I can manipulate the amount of spare time I want and can go swimming when it suits me or staying home when I feel the urge."

"What do you do, Greg that allows you so much freedom?" asked Myra. "The only ones I know who have so much freedom are drug lords and prostitutes, and even they might have certain restrictions placed on them.".

"I'm neither, Myra. I'm the owner of an IT company, and for fun, I'm a writer."

"But surely writing must be a difficult job in which to make money?" said Michael.

"It is for most writers, but I don't write for the money, I do it for the enjoyment and as a release from the daily pressures of life. The IT is the supplier of the income."

The drinks flowed, the food got devoured and the company was pleasant in its extreme. Myra was scintillating with her charm and wit, while Rob and Greg had swapped places on the couch and were now sitting next to each other, much to Myra's delight. Selwyn had moved to the floor at Michael's feet and was resting his head on Michael's knees. Everyone was relaxed. At midnight, the reality of there being another day ahead of them hit home.

"I'm sorry to be such a wet blanket," said Greg apologizing profusely, "but I have a plane to catch early tomorrow... sorry, this morning. I think I must be going, if you'll excuse me. It's been a wonderful evening and I must thank all of you for the great time I've had."

Selwyn and Michael got up to see Greg out, and immediately Rob also said that he should be going as well. The breaking up of the party seemed to be the sign for Myra to collect her things and also decide to leave. Selwyn took Michael aside and said that he thought Rob was going to use this opportunity to tell Greg about Gary and that he didn't think it advisable for Myra to leave with them because it might make Rob's task all that more difficult. Michael agreed and took his Mum to one side.

"Mum, why not stay a minute."

She looked puzzled. "But everyone's leaving and besides it's getting late."

Michael explained to her that they thought it better for Greg and Rob to leave at the same time, *in case they wanted to make arrangements to meet!*

"Oh, how silly of me," chuckled Myra, blushing at the thought of the two men making arrangements. "I spend all night trying to match them up and then I want to make their contacting each other problematic."

"Will you two be OK?" enquired Selwyn as they opened the front door.

"We'll be fine, thanks," said Rob, putting a hand on Greg's shoulder.

Greg smiled happily as he felt the sturdy hand rest on his shoulder.

"Now Greg, don't allow this man to merely put a hand on your shoulder," said Myra. "Make sure that he puts a ring on your finger."

Both Greg and Rob smiled at each other and then at Myra.

"We'll see what happens," replied Rob. "And thank you both for the lovely evening. I've really enjoyed myself, and Selwyn, don't be at work before 10:00 tomorrow. I think we'll all need to sleep in."

After their goodbyes, Greg and Rob went down in the elevator to their respective cars, but before they departed company, Rob told Greg he wanted to speak to him so he asked Greg if he wanted to go round to Rob's apartment and have a chat, to which Greg agreed.

Fifteen minutes later, Michael said, "Right Mum, now I think it's safe for you to leave, and should they still be downstairs, pretend you didn't see them and go straight home."

"He's such a demanding son, isn't he, Selwyn. Thanks to both of you for a wonderful evening and remember Selwyn, Michael promised you something tonight."

"I beg your pardon?" questioned Selwyn.

"Those sexy leather jeans, honey and what's in them!"

"Oh yes," laughed Selwyn, "I'll remind Michael. Bye Myra and thanks for spending the evening with us. We appreciated it."

Myra kissed both boys, hugged each and left for her journey home.

Chapter 16

Greg had followed Rob back to Rob's apartment and when they got upstairs, Rob had asked Greg if he wanted something to drink.

"I shouldn't really, but what the hell, just one night cap and then I'll call it a night," replied Greg.

"Beer do?"

"Sure that's fine."

Rob grabbed two beers from his fridge and took them back to the lounge where Greg was sitting waiting. He handed a beer to Greg and sat down next to him on the couch.

"Gee, it's a long time since we've had a moment to ourselves," pondered Rob.

"Sure is," echoed Greg.

"I missed you after we went our separate ways, Greg. I don't know, but after you left I often wondered whether I'd done the right thing and if I had, perhaps I was too proud to come back to you and ask if you wanted to get back together."

Greg smiled. "Funny you should say that, because I went through much the same frame of mind. Initially I was very hurt but then I put it down to fate. I thought that if we were meant for each other, our break up wouldn't have happened, but maybe I was wrong."

"After we broke up, did you meet anyone else?" asked Rob.

"I met a couple of guys, but it was more out of frustration than anything else. It just wasn't the same. You know the feeling, I'm sure."

"I know. I was the same. I went crazy for a short while, picking up anyone who took my fancy, but then I began to settle down and take stock of my life. It was about that time that I decided to open my own business as a P.I."

"And Michael and Selwyn; how did you meet them?" enquired Greg.

"Michael sold me this apartment and it was when he was talking to me that he said he had a friend who was looking for work, and as I was on my own, I offered him a job, so we've been friends for a relatively short time. And you?"

"Oh!" laughed Greg. "I cruised Selwyn at the swimming pool when he was there one day on his own. I liked the look of him and although he tried to rebuff me, I sensed that he'd give in, so we went back to their apartment. Nothing really happened because Michael came home earlier than expected."

"Oh wow! So what did you do?"

Greg chuckled almost uncontrollably. "Selwyn hid me under the dining room table."

Rob roared with laughter.

"You're having me on! Did Michael know you were hiding there?"

"No and so far as I know, he still doesn't know. I don't think Selwyn has ever told him."

"How did you get out without him finding you?"

"They were going to lunch so Selwyn told Michael to go down to the car and wait while he got dressed."

"You mean he never had any clothes on?"

"No, he still had on his Speedo."

"The mind boggles," chuckled Rob. "So then what happened?"

"I left and Selwyn got dressed."

"But then how did you meet Michael?"

"At the swimming pool again. He and Selwyn were both there and when Michael went in for a swim, I went and chatted to Selwyn. When Michael returned, Selwyn introduced us, but never mentioned that we'd met at the pool; he just said we were old friends."

"Oh."

"Then Michael invited me back to the apartment for drinks. After we'd had a few to drink, Michael and Selwyn were debating what their ideal type of man was and after much discussion, the three of us ended up having a bit of fun together, and I stayed the night."

"That sounds great. And now, do you have anyone in your life?" asked Rob, changing the tone of his inquiry.

"No," replied Greg almost sadly. "And you?"

"Same. All alone."

Both men looked solemnly into each other's eyes.

Greg smiled and added, "Two lonely old men."

"Lonely maybe, but not old. You look incredibly good for your age."

"Thanks, Rob, but then so do you."

Rob smiled and acknowledged the compliment. He stretched out a hand and laid it gently on Greg's thigh. "I really like you Greg. I always have."

Greg blushed, and placed a hand over Rob's. "The feeling's mutual."

Rob felt it was time to broach the topic of Gary.

"Greg, on a more serious note, I have to speak to you about Gary, your son."

"What about him, Rob?"

"You said that he'd phoned you today, or should I say yesterday," said Rob, looking at his watch and noting the time.

"Yes."

"And you remember I got that phone call at Michael and Selwyn's place."

"Yes."

"Well, that call was from Miami. Gary has been arrested because of a murder that took place in Miami and he's a suspect."

Greg looked startled but somehow not unduly shocked.

"The person who phoned me was my ex-wife who's with the cops down there and she told me that they had caught and arrested him."

"But what was your connection with Gary?"

"He had approached me to investigate his partner whom he'd said had gone to Miami and taken credit cards and money, among other things. The reason I went to Miami was to find his partner and see what was going on, but unfortunately, while I was down there the partner got shot and died, and so the police were looking for Gary, and for that matter, so was I."

"Rob, I can only thank you for putting me in the picture, but what can I do about it?"

"I'm going to go down to Miami with you in the morning. I'll get a ticket at the airport and the two of us can go and get Gary's situation sorted out, if that's OK with you?"

"I really appreciate your concern, but isn't it out of the way for you. You have a business to run."

"Greg, I told you that I liked you, which to me means, that I would be willing to do anything for you, and what I want to do is accompany you to Miami and help you at least get clarity on Gary's situation. In any case, I can now call on Selwyn to look after the office while I'm away."

Greg sat contemplating for a while then agreed to Rob accompanying him.

"Look, it's so late already, Greg, why not stay here the night, then in the morning we can leave from here and go straight to the airport. You can always wear something of mine if it fits you."

"Would you mind?"

"I've offered haven't I? You can have my bed and I'll sleep on the couch."

"I can't let you to do that."

"You have a choice; either the couch for you or for me, or we can sleep together in the bed! The choice is yours."

"I'll take the couch," replied Greg.

Rob's face was a picture of despondency and Greg could see it, so he recanted.

"OK, let's share the bed."

"That's more like it," said a gleeful Rob. "Then let's not waste time," he continued, grabbing Greg's hand and leading him off to the bedroom.

After undressing, they both climbed into bed alongside each other. Rob's arms encircled Greg and pulled him closer towards him as though to protect him, then they closed their eyes and slept, but only for a short period because Rob could feel his erection taking control and soon he was pushing his torso up tight against Greg's and both could feel the hardness between them. After a while, Rob took charge of the situation and began to remind Greg of their previous intimate moments together and soon Greg was moaning as Rob brought him to a high and both men climaxed together and then fell asleep again.

***

The sun rose bright and early and with it the ringing of a telephone that broke Michael and Selwyn's slumber.

"Who's phoning at this time of the morning," yawned a tired Michael. "Don't you want to get it Selwyn?"

"Not really, but I suppose I have to," he said, crawling from the warmth and comfort of the bed.

Selwyn staggered through to the lounge while the ringing became louder. He picked up the receiver and heard a cheery voice.

"Hello my darling. You promised to let me know what surprises Michael had in store for you last night."

Selwyn giggled loudly.

"I don't believe this. Myra, you're wicked. I'm not going to give you the juicy details of what we did after you left."

"But you promised."

"Let's just say, your son performed brilliantly. Is that OK?"

"That's what I like to hear, now go back to bed and have a great day. Bye."

With that the line went dead. Selwyn replaced the receiver and walked back to the bedroom in disbelief.

"Who was that?" shouted Michael.

"You won't believe it, it was your mother."

"So early! What the hell did she want?"

Again Selwyn giggled and climbed back into bed and cuddled up next to Michael.

"She wanted to know if we'd had sex last night," he whispered.

"You're not serious!"

"I am. Her words were 'what surprises did Michael have in store for you last night?'"

"And what did you say to her?"

"I told her you performed brilliantly."

"You didn't!"

"I did, and it's the truth."

"You know, you're as bad as my mother, but thanks."

Just as Selwyn was about to snuggle down to go to sleep again, the phone rang again.

"I hope that's not your mother again," he said, padding back into the lounge.

"Hello," said his tired voice.

"Selwyn, it's Rob. Sorry to have woken you up so early ..."

" ...oh don't worry you're not the first, Michael's Mum has already phoned this morning."

"What on earth for?"

"You won't believe it, to find out if Michael and I had sex last night."

Rob bellowed with laughter. "That mother of his is something else. No listen, I'm going to Miami with Greg this morning. In fact I'm phoning you from the airport, so you'll have to open the office today, OK?"

"No problem. Is he OK?"

"Yes, but I'll fill you in when I get back."

"Which is when?"

"I don't know but don't worry about us, we'll be fine. You just keep the business running."

"Hey listen, are you two trying to get back together?"

"I told you I'll fill you in when I get back. So cheers."

The phone went dead and Selwyn once again traipsed through to the bedroom.

"Who was that?"

"Rob. He and Greg are going to Miami together and I have to open the office. I think it sounds as though they might be making an effort to get back together."

"Good luck to them," said Michael, stretching and climbing from the warmth of the bed.

"Where are you going?" asked a pleading Selwyn.

"With all these interruptions, I might as well get up and get ready for work, and so should you, seeing that you now have to open the office."

"Ah, I thought we might have a lie-in."

"Forget it, it's time to get up, otherwise you'll be telling my mother how many times a day we have sex."

Chapter 17

In Miami, Greg and Rob hired a car and drove to a hotel to book a room and drop their bags. From there they headed to the police station at which Frankie was stationed in order to see Gary and speak to him.

"Do you often see your son, Greg?" asked Rob as they drove along the busy road.

"I suppose I don't see him as often as I should. How about you?"

"Same here. I haven't seen my boy for some time, but my excuse is that he's in California and it's a mission to get there. Also, he's big enough now not to be looked after, so I convince myself that I don't have to visit that often."

"I sometimes think it's sad that we don't worry too much about our kids once they get to the adult stage," continued Greg.

"Hey, don't feel too guilty. I think the same applies to them. How often do they come and visit their parents?"

"True."

"But you get on well with Gary don't you?"

"He's actually a good boy, so I don't understand this business."

"Don't worry as soon as we meet up with Frankie, we'll find out what's happening and take it from there."

They rounded a corner and headed into the grounds of the police station, alighted from their vehicle and went in to find Frankie. She was busy on a call at the time, but as soon as she was finished and saw Rob, she put down the phone and came hurrying over.

"Hi Frankie," said Rob, giving her a friendly kiss. "Frankie, this is Gary's Dad, Greg."

They greeted each other and Frankie took them into a secluded office where they could talk.

"What are you doing here, Rob? I thought you guys had gone back for good after your short visit to Miami?"

"Sure, Selwyn and I went back, but then I found out that Greg was Gary's father so I said I would accompany him down here."

Frankie looked at the two men and gave then a knowing smile, but never elaborated on why she had adopted that smile.

"Frankie, can you tell me exactly what's happened with Gary?" asked Greg.

"I don't know if Rob has filled you in with all the details leading up to his arrest...?"

"A little."

"Well, as you probably know, Gary's partner, Byron was shot and killed in the apartment that he was staying. On the night of the murder Byron was in the company of a hustler and they'd been smoking a joint. The hustler claims he saw nothing because according to him, it was too dark. That we have our doubts about. Gary had hired Rob to investigate Byron's behavior because according to Gary, Byron had disappeared with Gary's credit cards, jewelry and money. In investigating Byron, Rob came down to Miami and it was while he was here that the shooting took place, but after the shooting Rob said that he was convinced that he and Selwyn had seen Gary roaming around Miami. At one stage Selwyn gave chase, but unfortunately lost him, if it was him they'd seen. It was only later, after Rob and Selwyn had headed home, that we caught Gary and arrested him."

"Did he confess to the shooting?" asked Greg.

"Funnily enough, he hasn't confessed to anything. He keeps denying it, but we know that he had to have done it."

"On what evidence?" enquired Greg.

"We don't have the murder weapon, but based on the hustler's story, we can only deduce that it must have been Gary."

"But did the hustler say that Gary was in the apartment?"

"No, not in so many words."

"Can I see my boy?" asked Greg.

"Certainly. If you want to follow me, I'll take you to the holding cell."

"Do you mind if I go along?" asked Rob.

"Not at all," said Frankie, leading the way, "so long as Greg doesn't mind."

"No, I'd like Rob there."

The three headed down to the holding cell where Gary sat on the edge of a hard bench, his head in his hands. Frankie inserted the key and unlocked the door. Gary looked up and on seeing his father jumped up and flung his arms around Greg. Rob stood in the doorway and watched, along with Frankie.

Rob watched as father and son clasped each other tightly and thoughts of his own son flooded into his mind. How would he feel if it had been him standing there instead of Greg? Frankie excused herself and said she would be upstairs in her office, but there would be a policeman outside the cell to unlock when they were ready to leave. The cell door was locked again and Rob watched with interest and fascination as the two men hugged.

"Come Gary, let's sit down and tell me what happened," said Greg, his voice soothing and calm.

Rob stood in a corner listening to their conversations while father and son sat on the bench.

"I don't remember what happened," sobbed Gary. "I remember Byron and Brad being there, an argument and then fleeing when I heard the bang. I just ran, probably for my own safety."

"So you were there, like Frankie said, but did you hit Byron, Gary?"

"I might have, Dad, but I don't know, I just lost it."

At this point, Rob interrupted.

"Gary, if you intended to shoot Byron, where did you put the gun if you fled as you say?"

"But I don't remember carrying a gun."

"Well, there must have been a gun for Byron to have got shot. So either you had one or Brad had one."

"It certainly wasn't me. I honestly don't remember having one. I don't even possess one or have a license for one."

"Rob, you don't think it could have been an outsider who shot Byron? What I mean is a person could have been lurking outside and saw them through the window," asked Greg, trying to find some explanation for Byron's shooting.

"Look anything is possible, but Frankie didn't say anything along those lines when she spoke to me."

"Maybe they haven't thought of that aspect," suggested Greg.

"I suppose we can always suggest it to her and see what her thoughts are on that."

"Rob, be honest with me and tell me whether you think we aught to get a lawyer for Gary."

"I think let's ask Frankie, because I don't know whether they've actually laid formal charges against Gary."

"Would you mind finding out for me?" requested Greg.

"Not at all."

Rob called the guard to unlock the cell door and he made his way upstairs to Frankie's office.

"Frankie, sorry to disturb you, but Greg wants to know how serious the accusations are against Gary. Should he get a lawyer or is it still too early to say?"

"At the moment, I don't think you need worry as we haven't finalized our investigation and we can't find the weapon that fired the shots."

"Then I'll tell him not to worry unduly."

"Sure, but tell me," asked Frankie with a gleam in her eyes, "is there something serious between you and Greg?"

"Now what makes you think that?" grinned Rob, blushing as he said it.

"I was just wondering whether you had Greg in mind to settle down with, that's all."

"We'll have to see. We haven't seen each other for some years and then when you phoned we were both at Selwyn's birthday party. I didn't know that he was going to be there, and we got to chatting and one thing led to another. Also, Gary had hired me to find his partner, but I didn't know that they were father and son."

"You say you haven't seen him for some years; did you know him before?"

"Yes, we had a little fling once, but then we broke up."

"Before or after we were divorced?"

"You don't have to worry about that. It was well after."

As they spoke one of the other agents brought in Brad Knowles for further questioning. Frankie noticed this and asked Rob whether he thought Greg might want to see the 'other' guy.

"For what reason?" asked Rob.

"I just thought that he might want to see the guy who's implicated his son."

"I suppose there's no harm in asking him. Shall we go down and ask him?"

Frankie and Rob went back down to the cell where Greg was still sitting talking to Gary and asked him if he wanted to see Brad. Greg seemed a little reticent, but with some persuasion from Rob, he relented and agreed. They left Gary once more and headed back upstairs to an interview room where they could view Brad through some one-way glass, much like one would do in a line-up.

In a small room sat Brad with an investigating officer. Brad was still dressed as though he were on an outing to the beach; cut-off jeans and a string vest.

"That's him," said Rob pointing Brad out to his friend.

Greg never reacted. He remained transfixed. He stared long and hard at the young man in the string vest. They all stood listening to the line of questioning that the officer was asking. Brad answered much the same way that he had previously. If he was hiding anything, it was remaining hidden. At no stage did his answers vary from the previous interview.

After half an hour of constant questioning, the officer left the room and came around to where Frankie was standing.

"Seems to be the same answers, Frankie," said the officer, looking a little desperate.

It was then that Greg offered a suggestion.

"Do you think I could go in there and speak to him?"

Rob looked from Greg to Frankie, to see if she agreed.

"It's not customary, but I don't see any harm in that. However, you'll have to have an officer in there with you. I know it's not the norm to do this, but as your son's life is on the line, I think it'll be fine. Officer Brown," she said turning to a nearby officer, "will you take this man into the interviewing room with you please."

Frankie and Rob stood watching through the glass panel as Greg entered. Brad had been lying cradling his head on his arms as if trying to sleep. As the room door closed, Brad looked up. On seeing Greg, he became hysterical and shouted, "No, not you!"

"What's his problem?" muttered Rob.

Terror was written across Brad's face as he stared at Greg, shouting like a demented creature.

"Get him away from me. Get him out of here," screamed Brad.

The officer immediately took Greg out of the interview room as Frankie hurried around to the room door.

"Officer Brown, take him away from here please. Take him to my office and wait with him there until I come."

Rob watched through the glass window as Frankie entered the

interview room to pacify Brad.

"It's OK Brad, just calm down. He's gone. You're OK."

Brad was almost hyperventilating; his face was ashen and he was shaking with fear.

"Brad, why did you react to that man so dramatically?"

"I don't want to see him again."

"What do you mean 'see him again'? When have you seen him before?"

Brad's body shook and he continued to sob gently.

"Brad, answer me. Where do you know that man from?"

"It's him!'

"What do you mean, 'it's him'?"

"He's the one who had the gun."

Rob gasped when he heard this coming from Brad's mouth. He stared through the glass panel, unbelievingly. He looked carefully at the hustler in his tatty clothes and wondered whether this man was just trying to lay the blame at someone else's door. How could Greg have shot Byron? As far as everyone knew, Greg had been back home, but then Rob realized that he'd only seen Greg recently at Selwyn's party and that perhaps he had been in Miami all along.

"Brad, just calm down. He's gone. Tell me how he killed Byron," asked Frankie, quietly.

"I know it was him. I recognize him."

"But Brad, earlier you had said that it was dark and that you couldn't see. Now you're telling me that you saw him. Which story am I to believe?"

"I'm telling you the truth."

"Which truth, Brad. There are truths and truths and I don't know which one this is. Tell me why I should believe you now when you say you recognize him, yet early you decided that you hadn't seen anything? Perhaps you only recognize him as someone you might have picked up one evening."

In between half-hearted sobs, Brad tried to control himself and tell Frankie his story.

"It was him who fired the shot and killed Byron," he said in a calm, controlled voice, staring Frankie in the eyes as he said it.

"You're absolutely sure?" enquired Frankie.

"Yes."

His answer was firm and direct.

Rob, who had been almost holding his breath throughout all this, sighed in disbelief. If what Brad was saying was true, then Rob had been on the verge of going into a relationship with a murderer.

Frankie left Brad in the interview room and returned to Rob.

"I really am sorry you had to hear all this. I know that you have feelings for Greg, but if what Brad is saying is true, it's better to find out about him now rather than later."

It was evident that Rob had been shocked by what he'd heard, yet somehow, he didn't want to believe it.

"I still can't understand. Greg just doesn't seem the type to commit murder."

"And what type are those, Rob? How do you distinguish a murderer from a non-murderer? And don't tell from the look on their face. The truth is, we can't tell who murderers are and who are not, at least not until it happens. I'm going up to my office to speak to Greg about this whole business. Are you coming?"

Rob never answered, but dutifully followed Frankie as she made her way back upstairs. In her office sat Greg with the officer. Frankie and Rob walked in and closed the door behind them. Greg glanced up and saw them, then made eye contact with Rob. They both looked deeply into each other's eyes, then Greg hung his head.

"Greg do you want to tell me what happened the night that Byron got shot?"

Greg remained motionless.

Silence reigned.

"Greg do you feel that you need a lawyer?" persisted Frankie.

Still there remained silence from Greg.

"Greg I want to help you if I can," continued Frankie, "but if you remain silent, then I can't help you."

"Rob must go. I can't speak in front of him," whispered Greg.

Frankie nodded her head towards the door and Rob got the message. He quietly moved from the room and closed the door behind him. He felt hurt at being rejected in this manner because it was he who wanted to help Greg. This time there was no glass panel to look through and see or hear what was being discussed in the room. Rob paced up and down outside Frankie's office, like a caged tiger.

An hour later, Frankie emerged from her office looking solemn. She saw Rob, who had found a chair, and went over to him. She knelt beside him, looked him in the eyes and quietly said, "I'm sorry."

Rob had a pained expression and asked to see Greg.

"Not yet, Rob."

"Frankie, what did he say?"

"He admitted to shooting Byron..."

"...But he's not a killer."

"Not in the way most people think, Rob. He did kill, but for love."

"What do you mean?"

"He killed for the love of his son. In his opinion, Byron had been ripping Gary off and Greg didn't like seeing Gary hurt by this greedy young man ...

"... So he took matters into his own hands."

"Yes, you said it, Rob. I think that Gary, in some strange way, although not guilty, was ready to take the rap for his father, but I'm sure that sooner or later, Greg would have come clean and acknowledged that he'd done it."

"Frankie, please let me see him, even if it's just to say goodbye."

Frankie sensed that Rob had made an unconscious decision that he was going to leave Miami and Greg and go home forever, so she led Rob into the office where Greg sat solemnly subdued and left the two men together. Rob went over to him and sat down in front of him. The two men made eye contact.

"I'm sorry Rob," said calm, but subdued Greg. "I don't know whether you'll ever understand why I did it, but I hope that one day, you being a father, you might have the goodness and knowledge in your heart to understand. Doing it was painful for me, but seeing how he treated my son was also painful, and I couldn't allow that to go on."

Greg sobbed a couple of times, but fought on with his explanation.

"I don't expect your sympathy; all I hope for is your understanding, if that's possible. Love is an extremely strong emotion and although I have love for you in my heart, I'll understand your not wanting anything to do with me. When we met, fate intervened and we parted like two ships passing on a rough sea; now today, those same two ships docked in a harbor where they felt safe from emotional storms, but on leaving the harbor, fate has once more intervened. I hope that one day soon you will find someone with whom you can share all that love that you have to offer and that the person will bring the happiness that is due to you, but above all, don't forget your love for those close to you."

Rob remained silent. He couldn't reply. He felt empty, unable to grasp the whole incident, but he'd listened intently to every word that Greg had spoken. The wound was too raw to understand just now, but perhaps in days to come, he might gather understanding.

Greg stretched out a hand, offering it to Rob, who stared at it at first, then stretched out his own hand and took Greg's and held it firmly. They remained like this for a moment and then Rob moved to the door to Frankie's office and exited.

Chapter 18

Selwyn and Michael stood anxiously waiting at the airport for the flight from Miami to arrive. The tinny voice announced the plane's arrival over the speakers and waiting loved-ones edged closer to the arrivals gate to catch a glimpse of the persons they were waiting for. Michael and Selwyn strained their eyes to see the passengers coming through after they had collected their luggage.

"There he is," shouted Michael.

Michael and Selwyn pushed past the crowd and headed in the direction of their friend.

"Rob, are you OK?" enquired Selwyn as he reached the burly man.

"Hi! What are you guys doing here?"

"Rob, we're really sorry to hear about Greg," commiserated Michael, "but Frankie phoned us and told us what had happened, so we decided to come to the airport to meet you. We hope that you don't mind?"

"Gee, thanks, guys I really appreciate it," replied a depressed Rob.

It was late afternoon when the plane had landed so Selwyn and Michael decided that Rob would go back to their apartment for something to eat and have a drink, as well as put the two friends in the picture, as they were also finding it hard to believe.

As they drove through the afternoon traffic, Rob tried to come to terms with Greg's situation as he explained to Selwyn and Michael what had happened.

"Do you really believe he did it for love?" asked Michael.

"It was a shock at first. In fact it was wholly unbelievable, but I believe him, Mike. I understand now how he must have felt for Gary. There's also another side to this whole business; we don't know what happened in Gary's and Byron's relationship. Perhaps Byron was taking Gary for a real ride and was ripping him off as well as two-timing him, and Greg got to hear of it, and that might have made matters worse. I don't know if we'll ever find out the real truth. Perhaps in the court case they might, but I made a decision in Miami, that I wasn't going to attend the court case."

"Not?" asked Selwyn.

"No. I think it would upset me even more. I respect and believe Greg's story, but I still maintain that there are bits missing that we might never find out about."

"Rob, do you think if this hadn't happened you might have got together with Greg again?" enquired Michael.

"Yes, I think so. In fact I'm sure we would have because we both felt for each other, but then, as I've always found in my life, fate intervenes. You see, Selwyn, I told you relationships were bad things for me."

"Don't look at it like that. I know that somewhere, sometime, you'll find mister right," said Selwyn, trying to console Rob.

They arrived back at the apartment, opened the door and smelt the fragrant aroma of exotic spices.

"Something smells nice," chirped Rob, trying to lighten his heavy heart.

"It should, we hired a very good chef to cook dinner for us tonight as a special treat for you."

"At whose cost, Mike?"

"At great expense to your company. Let me introduce you to Chef Bloomberg."

As they walked into the kitchen, there stood Myra over the stove, smiling and cooking happily.

She flung her arms around Rob and hugged him.

"My darling I really am sorry to hear about Greg. It came as a shock to all of us when Michael told me, but you must be strong Rob; we're all here for you."

"Thanks Myra. I don't know what I'd do without friends like you, but I think I have a little more clarity in my mind about my relationship with Greg. We're not meant for each other, but life must go on, mustn't it?"

"Rob, don't you worry about a thing, my friends don't call me the Fixer for the Shicksas," said Myra confidently. "Michael keeps getting embarrassed by the way I try to match people up and I'll soon have a match for you."

"Mum you're doing nothing of the sort. Rob is big enough to make his own decisions."

"Sure he can make his own decisions, but that only comes after I've found him someone to decide on."

"At the moment, Myra, I don't think I want to be with anyone, present company excluded."

"Don't you worry about a thing, Rob. Relationships are like riding a horse; when you fall off, you get straight back on and carry on, and that's what you must do. Don't spend time moping around. Now listen, my friend Edith Berkovitz's son is a doctor, a urologist in fact. You couldn't ask for anything nicer than a good Jewish doctor. Now he's single and I think you two would be good for each other."

"Mum! You're at it again," reprimanded Michael.

"Sorry."

However, Myra's intentions were good and she couldn't bare to see unhappiness, so she strove on.

"If you're not into doctors, Mona Abraham's son is a lawyer and he's single. That might actually be a better bet for you because you're both in a similar business, dealing with crime and things."

"Mum, you're exasperating. Rob will find his own partner if he wants one and when he wants one, so enough!"

"I'm just trying to help."

"Mum, we appreciate your intentions, but I think you should spend all that energy into cooking the dinner. Come Rob, let's get you out of this den of iniquity and into the lounge. I'm sure you could do with a drink."

Selwyn and Michael led Rob back into the lounge where they got him a beer and told him to relax. Selwyn decided to try to take Rob's mind off the trauma of Miami.

"How about the three of us going away this weekend?" suggested Selwyn.

"That's a good idea," said an excited Michael. "We haven't been away for a while, but where did you have in mind, Selwyn?"

"I don't know. Anywhere, but away from here. Would you like that Rob?"

"Maybe it'll do me good to get my mind off things and get away. Yes, I would like that."

"Then that's it. This weekend we're heading out into the country or off to the coast. You choose."

"I really don't mind," repeated Rob.

"Let's head to the coast," suggested Michael, "I think a bit of fresh air will clear our heads of all the crap that's been happening here."

"Right, then the coast it is."

"Dinner is served," shouted the visiting chef, from the kitchen. "Come and get it!"

The men traipsed back into the kitchen and helped bring the plates and dishes to the dining room table where they sat down to an exotic Thai stir-fry meal with fragrant rice.

Although Michael and Selwyn tried to steer the conversation away from Greg and the relationship between Greg and Rob, dear loving Myra was persistent in trying to get Rob hitched up with someone, anyone, in an effort to bring happiness into his life. Eventually Rob turned to Myra and said, "I am grateful for your effort, Myra, but I know that I'm not relationship material, so don't try so hard."

"Mum, if Rob wants to go into a relationship, you'll be the first to know and then you can start networking, so in the meantime, leave off. Deal?"

"Deal," replied a reluctant Myra, "but you have to promise me that you'll come to me and I'll vet the person to see if I think he's good enough for you."

"I promise, Myra," said a smiling Rob.

From then on, the dinner went off without any talk of relationships or of Greg and the four thoroughly enjoyed their evening. After they had finished their meal, Myra insisted that the boys stay with Rob while she washed up, and once she had completed that, she excused herself and said that she was heading home.

"I'll leave you boys to chat together, but remember Rob, if you need anything, just give us a call."

"I will Myra, and thank you for all your love and care."

Rob kissed Myra on the cheek, causing her to blush and then she left the apartment on a high, gently rubbing her cheek where Rob had kissed her.

"I think you've made my Mum's night, Rob."

"She really has a good heart, Mike, so you mustn't get too upset when she goes on about her match-making."

"It's just that sometimes it becomes embarrassing."

"Just remember, you only have one biological mother, so enjoy her and love her while you can."

As Rob began to relax more, Selwyn asked if he wanted to stay the night at their apartment.

"I can't impose on you guys. You've already shown me too much care. No, I'll be fine."

"You are not imposing, you are more than welcome to stay, if you like," reiterated Michael.

"I'm sure that you'd rather be with friends than on your own, especially after what you've been through."

"Thanks Selwyn, but I'll be fine. In fact, I think I should be making my way home."

Michael and Selwyn reluctantly bundled Rob into their car and headed to Rob's apartment, where they safely deposited him.

"I'll see you in the morning," shouted Selwyn as they drove off into the night, leaving Rob to his thoughts.

Chapter 19

Selwyn and Michael packed their vehicle for the weekend at the coast and set off to pick up Rob, who was waiting on the curb for them. Since Rob's return from Miami, as each day passed, so he became a little more accepting of the situation he had found himself in, and with having Selwyn constantly in the office to 'keep an eye on him', he had begun to become his old self again.

"Where are we going?" asked Rob once he had got into the car.

"Fire Island," quipped Selwyn.

Michael grinned.

"Are you serious?" enquired Rob, sounding concerned.

"No, I'm only joking," laughed Selwyn, turning to Rob who was sitting in the rear of the car. "We're taking you to a secluded part of the coast where a colleague of Michael's has a beach cottage."

"That sounds nice; away from the madding crowd, so to speak."

"That's it," continued Selwyn, "just the three of us. Now how romantic is that!"

Rob laughed along with Michael and Selwyn.

"I couldn't have asked for two more romantic people to share a weekend with, than you two."

"Oh, you might regret it," said Selwyn, flippantly. "You don't know how romantic we can get, not so Michael?"

"Absolutely," came the reply from the driver.

Throughout the journey they chatted freely about everything and anything, other than Greg. The landscape changed as they headed away from the city and out into the country. It was pleasant to see such greenery abounding and once they hit the coastal road, it brought a sense of excitement when they saw the sea. Selwyn was like an excited child, bouncing up and down in his seat with excitement, when he first caught a glimpse of the tranquil blue water.

Michael jokingly told him that should he behave himself in the car, he'd be allowed to make sand castles when he got to the beach. This excited Selwyn even more, acting out very much like a young child would. This enhanced jollity made their journey all the more relaxing and fun, and soon Rob was joining in teasing Selwyn.

They moved from the main coast road and went along a gravel side road that led down towards the direction of the sea. As they neared the actual water, they caught sight of a wooden chalet, which was to be their home for the weekend. Michael drove up to the cottage and parked the car alongside of it. All three scrambled out. Michael took in a deep breath and then exhaled slowly.

"Hm! Smell that sea air," he said, taking in a few more deep breaths.

All three stood looking out over the flat ocean. Flat it might have been, but there were gentle swells, which formed and then rolled slowly landwards to fall onto the shore. From the layout of the beach, they could see that there was a gentle slope from the sand into the water, so they knew that there was unlikely to be strong currents or sudden drops in the ocean floor. Just the right type of beach to be able to go quite far out yet still be able to touch the sea bottom.

"Come on guys, let's unpack and then we can head down there for a swim," hollered Michael.

The car was hastily unloaded and they made their way into the cottage. It was simply furnished, yet clean. There were two bedrooms, a lounge and kitchen. A bathroom, fitted with a shower and toilet, was situated next to the main bedroom, and off the front door was a small patio on which one could sit and watch the sun set.

Bags and suitcases were hurriedly unpacked and foodstuff was placed in the kitchen, along with the beers.

"Come on, let's go for a swim," cajoled Selwyn.

Michael and Selwyn took the main bedroom while Rob had the other, and soon they were all slipping on their bathing costumes. Michael and Selwyn emerged in their Speedos and waited in the lounge for Rob.

"Come on Rob, you're slow for a young man," chirped Selwyn.

Rob emerged from his room, in a pale blue Speedo. Although Selwyn had seen Rob naked, Michael had never seen Rob with his shirt off, let alone any other clothes. He smiled admiringly at the giant man's well-developed body and the tightly fitting Speedo that enhanced its contents. Selwyn nudged Michael and reprimanded him for staring.

"I'm sorry, it's just that I've never seen Rob like this. He's got a pretty good body," he muttered to Selwyn. Although Michael never said it, he also admired the fully packed bulge in the front of Rob's Speedo.

The three ran down onto the sand and into the cool, refreshing sea where they splashed around and dived under the swells as they approached. There was total relaxation among them and Selwyn and Michael noticed how much Rob was enjoying himself. It was clear to them that Rob's mind was focused on the here and now and wasn't dwelling on the progress that was taking place in Miami.

That evening, after they had showered and changed, they decided to have a barbecue on the front lawn that led to the beach. Michael and Rob made a fire while Selwyn busied himself in the kitchen making salads for them. Soon everything was ready and the three of them, along with their drinks, sat down in the dying warmth of the setting sun to eat their dinner. As the sun set, a golden glow fell on the sea, lightening the sky to an orange color.

"Wow, what a beautiful sunset," remarked Michael, in awe of what he saw. "You never see these sorts of sunsets back home, that's why I enjoy heading out of town sometimes."

"Actually, we should do this more often," suggested Selwyn.

As the sun set and the darkness began to encompass the men and their cottage, they moved indoors, having eaten, put out their fire and collected the dirty plates and dishes. They all made their way to the kitchen to help wash up and tidy the place, then they settled in the lounge.

"There's no TV here, so what would you like to do?" enquired Michael.

"What about a game of cards? Let's play poker," said Selwyn, and then added, "how about strip poker?"

Both Michael and Rob chuckled.

"Trust you to say that," said Michael.

"I don't mind, if you want to," said Rob, who was now totally relaxed.

Selwyn immediately jumped up, ran to the bedroom to fetch the cards which he had brought with him, and hurried back.

"Right, simple rules," he said, shuffling the deck of cards. "Whoever loses must remove a piece of clothing. Rob, I hope you're not very good at poker," he added.

"You'll never know until you play," came the reply.

"All I know is that I'm useless at this game," volunteered Michael.

"Oh good, we'll have you naked in no time," laughed Selwyn. "Oh, and another thing, whoever is left the winner, gets breakfast in bed tomorrow morning. Agreed?"

Rob and Michael grinned at the suggestion.

"Fine, agreed," they both said.

Selwyn dealt the first hand and the game was underway.

By a stroke of luck, more than anything else, Michael won the first game and was left still fully clothed, much to Selwyn and Rob's dismay.

After five rounds, Rob was down to his jeans and T-shirt, having removed his shoes and socks, while Selwyn had also lost a number of items.

"This is taking too long," whined Selwyn, "we've all still got too much on. I think we should have to take two items off if you lose," he suggested, but both Michael and Rob outvoted him, so the rules remained unchanged.

Michael went through a patch of bad luck and lost his shirt and shorts and was left sitting in his white briefs, while Rob, although having lost his shirt still wore his jeans. Selwyn, on the other hand seemed to be doing well and had decided to lose his shorts but keep his shirt on.

By 10:30 in the evening, and many beers later, Michael sat naked along with Rob, while Selwyn, although he'd chosen to lose his briefs, still had on his shirt.

"I win," shouted Selwyn with glee. "It's breakfast in bed for me tomorrow, so you two will have to get up early and start preparing.

Although the game had come to an end, the three remained as they were, in a state of undress. They were now either lazing on the floor or leaning against some piece of furniture.

Michael turned to Rob and said, possibly without thinking, "I think you've got the most magnificent body I've seen on a guy."

"Thanks Mike."

"No. I'm serious. Don't you think so, Selwyn?"

"Absolutely."

"You two are too kind. But you know, you guys are no pushover. I think you've also got good trim physiques."

The compliments continued to flow, just as much as the drink did. At one stage, Selwyn sidled up to Rob and placed his arms around the gentle giant and hugged him.

"I think he's sexy," slurred Selwyn, "don't you think so, Michael?"

Michael burped and then concurred with his partner.

"I could quite easily whip him off to bed," said Selwyn, continuing his appreciation of Rob's attributes, "couldn't you Michael?"

Michael smiled at Selwyn and Rob, then he looked down between his thighs and burst out laughing.

"What's the joke?" asked Selwyn.

Michael rolled onto his back and displayed his erection to the others. "Don't you think this answers your question?" he laughed.

Selwyn pretended to be disgusted by Michael's erotic situation, but Rob merely laughed along with the other two.

"I think we should all go to bed, together," said Michael standing up and taking Selwyn and Rob by the hand, all the while his erection bounced through the air like a periscope in search of a target to sink.

The three of them staggered to the main bedroom where they crashed onto the double bed and began to make love to each other.

Both Michael and Selwyn had a yearning to have Rob make love to them and so it became a battle of wills and desires as the two lovers fought to gain favor with Rob.

Rob, on the other hand also had his desires and although he had already had sex with Selwyn in Miami, it was now Michael that he wanted to possess.

"I want to see you make love to Selwyn," said Rob, encouraging Michael to dominate his partner.

Michael was only too willing to oblige because he enjoyed making love to Selwyn and within minutes, he had slid his hefty cock deep into Selwyn. Both men were panting and moaning as Michael thrust hastily in and out of Selwyn's tight ass. Then Rob decided it was time for him to join in.

Rob got himself a condom, unsheathed it onto his long, thick cock, lubed his lengthy dick and Michael's ass, and then aimed it at the throbbing entrance. Slowly Rob sank into Michael's warm chute, causing his young friend to gasp as the thickness began to spread his chute wider until Rob had sunk his cock deep into Michael so that his balls slapped against Michael's buns.

As the three men lay connected to one another, their movement built up to a unified rhythm and all three were panting, gasping and sweating together. This continued for what seemed an eternity until Selwyn gasped and warned them that he was close to shooting his load. Michael increased his thrusts and in doing so, so did Rob. As Selwyn fired the first of his shots, so Michael began emptying his load into Selwyn. Rob felt the tightness of Michael's ass strangle his shaft and he thrust long and deep into his friend as he too fired salvo after salvo of warm come.

As the three came slowly back from their high, their bodies began to relax and soon they were falling asleep.

***

The early morning sun blazed in through the window, hitting the three naked men, sprawled across the double bed and waking them. There were groans from hangovers and much yawning. Slowly they came to their senses and saw their situation.

"What a night!" exclaimed Rob, who was lying between Selwyn and Michael. "That was probably the best medicine for me. Thanks you guys."

They slowly wormed their way out of bed and went off, one by one to the bathroom to freshen up.

"Don't forget you two have to make breakfast for me," shouted Selwyn who was trying to stay in bed, but was being constantly nudged out by either Rob or Michael.

"Come on Mike, we did promise, but do we have to dress?"

"I can't see why, after all there's no one near this cottage and it's only us," said Michael wandering through to the kitchen, closely followed by Rob.

"Thanks for last night, Rob, you were great."

"My pleasure. Believe it or not, but from the time I first met you, I've had this desire to bed you and when Selwyn and I …"

"…It's OK, I know about you two in Miami."

"Did he tell you?"

"Yes, but not all the juicy details."

"Well, as I was saying when we had our little scene he had said you'd only do something if it were the three of us, because he told me about you two and Greg."

"I know it sounds funny," said Michael, but unless it's absolutely unavoidable, I never want to go with another guy unless Selwyn is also there."

"I know what you mean, but I don't understand what you mean by when it's unavoidable. Do you mean if someone raped you?"

"Not really. I had an incident when you and Selwyn were away. I had to take a client to a property with his mother. Obviously nothing happened, but after we left he phoned and said that he wanted to view the property again, so I went back. This time he was alone, so we went in and in this particular property there was a Jacuzzi…"

"…Oh lovely, I've always wanted to do it in a Jacuzzi."

"Well he filled the Jacuzzi with water and then we sat in there soaking. One thing led to another and soon we were making more than bubbles."

"Lucky you, or should I say, lucky him."

"But I've never told Selwyn about it."

"Now you have," said a voice behind them.

"Selwyn!" exclaimed a shocked Michael. "I didn't know you were there."

"It doesn't matter. I'm glad that you went with someone because it doesn't make me feel so bad then."

"But where does that sort of thing put your relationship, Selwyn?" asked Rob.

"I just believe that Michael's and my love for each other is strong enough to withstand anything and that includes people who might try to bust us up. I know that if I go with a guy, it's just to relieve my immediate frustrations, but when I get home I also know that I've got a loving, caring person waiting for me. If he wants to tell me that he's been with someone, that's his choice because I know I won't be jealous, I just feel closer to him because I realize that others find him attractive, but can't have him forever."

Rob looked deeply into Selwyn's eyes.

"You're quiet philosophical for someone so young."

"Now do you see why I said that being in a relationship can be good, and that's why I wish you could find someone that you could spend your life with?" remarked Selwyn.

"Maybe one day it will happen," said Rob, almost in a whisper.

The balance of the week end was spent sun tanning and swimming, but as no one other than the three of them was about, most of their activities were carried out in the nude. They gave themselves up to nature and enjoyed the total freedom given to them by the isolation of their cottage and the freedom expressed by each of the men. Rob felt a load lifted from his shoulders as he swam and ran up and down the beach.

"You know what I like about this weekend," he remarked to Michael at lunch time, "is the total freedom you and Selwyn have given to me. I've been able to be myself without comment or criticism and I'm really happy about that. The fact that I can be myself with you two guys gives me reason to live, not that I'm contemplating anything, but it allows me the opportunity to view life from another perspective."

Michael smiled knowing that he and Selwyn had managed to get through to Rob and show him that they were genuine friends, not just two people who might be on the take.

"And you know what else I'm really grateful for? It's your mother."

"My mother!"

"Yes, if it weren't for her sense of humor and her caring for me, I think I would have remained depressed for a much longer time. Appreciate her, Mike."

"I do."

"I know you do as her son, but you need to appreciate her for her inner soul. She is one of the most incredibly kind people I have met and her willingness to help others goes beyond the call of duty expected from a parent."

"You make me feel guilty, Rob."

"It's not my intention, Mike. I know you love her, but don't ever be embarrassed by her good intentions, even if they might seem a little bizarre. She's a good woman and you're lucky to have her. In fact, you must count your blessing on having not only a caring mother like Myra, but also for having Selwyn."

"I do, Rob. And believe me, I also count my blessings that I have a friend like you, and I appreciate everything you've done for Selwyn. If it hadn't been for you, he'd probably have driven me up the wall through his boredom, but you giving him a job also meant that he could cut back on his evening performances."

"Talking of that, I still have to see his complete act. You realize that I've never seen it from beginning to end."

"Well that you'll have to speak to him about."

"Selwyn!" shouted Rob from the front patio of the cottage to the lithe sun tanned body lying on the sand. "You owe me something."

Selwyn raised his head and looked up to the cottage.

"What?"

"I still haven't seen your act from beginning to end. When am I going to see it.?"

Selwyn laughed to himself. "I don't do it any more."

"Not at all?" asked Rob, sounding somewhat disappointed by the remark.

"Only special performances. You know private showings!"

"Do I qualify for a private showing?" enquired Rob.

"We'll have to see about that," came the tired reply.

"What do I need to qualify for a private showing?" asked Rob.

"I only do it in my home and for people whom I like, but they'll have to pay well."

"I can do that, if I qualify."

"Show me your money," replied Selwyn, now grinning from ear to ear at the banter he and Rob were having.

"Will this do?" asked Rob, thrusting his naked hips at Selwyn and in the process allowing his large cock to sway freely back and forth.

Selwyn giggled and replied, "only if my partner says that equates to the correct currency valuation."

Rob and Michael smiled and then laughed heartily at Selwyn's sense of humor. They had become good friends and they knew that they could depend on each other for support.

As the weekend drew to a close, the three men were saddened to be leaving, but they knew that there had been a bonding between them; a bringing together of similar minds and they knew that no matter what happened, they would always remain the best of friends because of their honesty and trust.

A Boner Book

Chapter 20

Back in the humdrum world of commerce and crime, the world of work and stress, the place where life waited for no one but rushed by, Selwyn, Michael and Rob cemented their friendship. The bonds between them were drawn closer together and they almost became a permanent threesome. Wherever one was, the other two were not far away, on most occasions, except if Selwyn was looking for someone with whom to have a quick sexual encounter.

Myra had taken to Rob and never gave up looking for the ideal partner for him, no matter how much he tried to dissuade her; in fact she flooded his life with men from doctors to lawyers, accountants to businessmen and she even found a Jewish plumber, a rarity in a world of professionals.

"A plumber, Mum! What does Rob want with a plumber? I thought you were aiming for one of the professionals?"

"Michael, Marc Cohen is not only very good-looking, but is also a very good plumber. He sorted out my waterworks and besides, he looks good when he takes off his shirt to work, and you must see how sexy he looks with his tool belt hanging low on his hips!"

"Then if you like him so much, Mum, why don't you keep him for yourself?"

"No, my darling, I think he'd be better for Rob, after all, I'm not looking for a permanent arrangement. No one could replace your father on a permanent basis – part-time, maybe!"

However, after all was said and done, Rob did date Marc the plumber, more to make Myra happy than himself, but he did later admit to Selwyn and Michael that Marc was a hunk, physically, but lacked the mental ability that Rob would have preferred.

As for Greg – the court case was held in Miami and Rob, as he had promised, didn't attend, but Frankie phoned him regularly to update him of the daily happenings, although Rob had said he didn't want to know.

Gary was released after a day of interrogation and so was Brad. However the judge in the case did reprimand Brad for attempting to defeat the ends of justice, and as for Greg, well he got six years. To some it may seem lenient, but the judge had said that owing to the circumstances and because of Greg's devotion to and protection of his son, he was going to give a reduced sentence, which pleased most of those who had an interest in the case.

***

Two years have gone by and Greg hasn't contacted Rob, but then Rob would probably ignore any communication from Greg, should it arrive. Rob, although he had strong feelings for Greg decided that bringing back the past was not an option and it was better to get on with his life and his business. As for the others, Selwyn and Michael are still happily ensconced in Michael's apartment, where on rare occasions, Selwyn will give a performance of his drag act, especially to Rob, and he is still happily employed by Rob as his right-hand-man. Myra is networking among her friends to see if she can't gain a reputation as a match-maker for the rich and famous, but the boys think it's more to satisfy Myra's own pleasures of being with younger men.

There have been some cases on which Rob has worked where he has involved both Selwyn and Michael and the three have continued to have their evenings of 'fun' together. However, they are all happy and busy sharing as much time together as they can, waiting for the next adventure in their lives, after all, fate can play some nasty twists sometimes.

About the Author

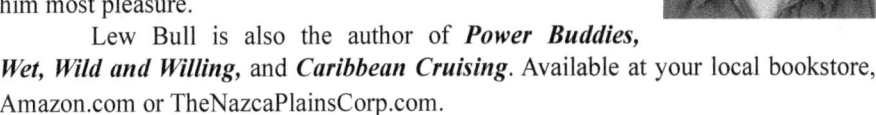

Lew Bull, who lives in Johannesburg, South Africa, has been published in a number of anthologies including, among others, *Ultimate Gay Erotica 2007* and *2008, Treasure Trail, Fast Balls, Travelrotica and Travelrotica Vol. 2, Don't Ask, Don't Tie Me Up, Cruise Lines* and *My First Time Vol. 5.*

Although he is involved in education, and has a Doctorate in this field, it is writing and traveling that brings him most pleasure.

Lew Bull is also the author of **Power Buddies, Wet, Wild and Willing,** and **Caribbean Cruising**. Available at your local bookstore, Amazon.com or TheNazcaPlainsCorp.com.